GRIMMS' FAIRY TALES

TRANSLATED
BY
MRS. EDGAR LUCAS

ILLUSTRATED
BY
ARTHUR
RACKHAM

PARENTS' MAGAZINE'S CULTURAL INSTITUTE
A Division of Parents' Magazine Enterprises, Inc.
New York

1966 Printing

Special contents copyright © MCMLXIV by Parents' Magazine Enterprises, Inc.
Printed in the United States of America

Library of Congress Catalog Card Number: 64-15714

PREFACE

Folklore began when early humanity wanted Right to win over Wrong, but had no means of bringing it about except in stories it could invent. Folk tales therefore have no known authors or origins. They were passed along from generation to generation by word of mouth. Down through the ages they have preserved much truth about life, not as it ever was, but as perhaps it could be. The primitive justice that ruled in these old tales brought joy to mankind. In them the too-powerful were toppled, the wicked were snared, and the humble rose to majesty. Centuries ago, when earth's people were downtrodden, that magic was their solace.

It would be hard to estimate the contribution to folk-tale literature made by the Brothers Grimm. Their deeply rooted German stories are more rugged and elemental than those of neighbor nations. France's Charles Perrault was the preceding collector and the true parent of European folklore. In the eighteenth and nineteenth centuries four other scholars achieved distinction similar to the Grimms': Joseph Jacobs and Andrew Lang in England; and in Norway, Peter Christian Asbjörnsen and Jörgen E. Moe. This small company saved for posterity the earliest make-believe of our western civilization.

Jakob and Wilhelm Grimm were men of learning who felt the profound worth of their native folk tales. Jakob was born in 1785, Wilhelm in 1786, in the German province of Hesse-Cassel. They belonged to a good family, but the five children with their widowed mother had been left in poverty. There was deep devotion in their home, and a special attachment between these brothers. Jakob, a student of language and grammar, became the great philologist of his country. His passion for the sound, meaning, and history of *words* led him eventually to his study of folklore. Wilhelm was much like his brother in character and appearance. He and his wife and children shared their happy home with Jakob, so the brothers' close relationship ended only when Wilhelm died in 1859. Jakob lived four years longer, but the great German dictionary on which they worked together was left incomplete.

For thirteen years Jakob and Wilhelm followed every folklore trail they could discover, and transcribed stories exactly as they heard them. To their colleagues these tasks seemed unworthy of such eminent professors. They collected tales "as if they were running after butterflies," asking men and women to remember those they had heard as children; catching the live tales before they perished in the minds of old folks. The Grimms were aware, of course, that different versions of a story appear in many places. Thus the French "Cinderella" and "Sleeping Beauty" recorded by Perrault corresponded to the German "Ashenputtel" and "Briar Rose." No one authentic "Cinderella" exists, for it has a dozen variations, some, as in Grimm, without the familiar pumpkin coach.

The Grimms owed their largest debt to Frau Katerina Viehmannin, an elderly peasant woman with a "perfect genius for storytelling." She lived in a nearby village, and the brothers often went to her house to hear and record. There they put on paper for the first time the forest depths and dark enchantments, the moody witches and clever animals of their fairy tales. They never softened a story's rough texture or refined its cruel fate.

Altogether they collected 210 stories which were published in two volumes in 1812 and 1815, as *Nursery and Household Tales*. Thirty-two favorite stories chosen for this collection could have been lost forever without the Grimms, who searched for them, and made them part of our classic literature.

IRENE SMITH
Former Superintendent of Work with Children
Brooklyn Public Library
Brooklyn, New York

CONTENTS

THE VALIANT TAILOR

A TAILOR was sitting on his table at the window one summer morning. He was a good fellow, and stitched with all his might. A peasant woman came down the street, crying, "Good jam for sale; good jam for sale."

This had a pleasant sound in the Tailor's ears; he put his pale face out of the window, and cried, "You'll find a sale for your wares up here, good Woman."

The Woman went up the three steps to the Tailor, with the heavy basket on her head, and he made her unpack all her pots. He examined them all, lifted them up, smelt them, and at last said, "The jam seems good; weigh me out four ounces, good Woman, and should it come over the quarter pound, it will be all the same to me."

The Woman, who had hoped for a better sale, gave him what he asked for, but went away cross, and grumbling to herself.

"That jam will be a blessing to me," cried the Tailor; "it will give me strength and power." He brought his bread out of the cupboard, cut a whole slice, and spread the jam on it. "It won't be a bitter morsel," said he, "but I will finish this waistcoat before I stick my teeth into it."

He put the bread down by his side, and went on with his sewing, but in his joy the stitches got bigger and bigger. The smell of the jam rose to the wall, where the flies were clustered in swarms, and tempted them to come down, and they settled on the jam in masses.

"Ah! who invited you?" cried the Tailor, chasing away his unbidden guests. But the flies, who did not understand German, were not to be got rid of so easily, and came back in greater numbers than ever. At last the Tailor came to the end of his patience, and seizing a bit of cloth, he cried, "Wait a bit, and I'll give it you!" So saying, he struck out at them mercilessly. When he looked, he found no fewer than seven dead and motionless. "So that's the kind of fellow you are," he said, admiring his own valour. "The whole town should know of this."

In great haste he cut out a belt for himself, and stitched on it, in big letters, "Seven at one blow!" "The town!" he then said, "the whole world shall know of it"; and his heart wagged for very joy like the tail of a lamb. The Tailor fastened the belt round his waist, and wanted to start out into the world at once; he found his workshop too small for his valour. Before starting, he searched the house to see if there was anything to take with him. He only found an old cheese, but this he put into his pocket. By the gate he saw a bird entangled in a thicket, and he put it into his pocket with the cheese. Then he boldly took to the road, and as he was light and active, he felt no fatigue. The road led up a mountain, and when he reached the highest point, he found a huge Giant sitting there comfortably looking around him.

The Tailor went pluckily up to him, and addressed him.

"Good-day, Comrade, you are sitting there surveying the wide world, I reckon. I am just on my way to try my luck. Do you feel inclined to go with me?"

The Giant looked scornfully at the Tailor, and said, "You jackanapes! you miserable ragamuffin!"

"That may be," said the Tailor, unbuttoning his coat and showing the Giant his belt. "You may just read what kind of fellow I am."

The Giant read, "Seven at one blow," and thought that it was people the Tailor had slain; so it gave him a certain amount of respect for the little fellow. Still he thought he would try him; so he picked up a stone and squeezed it till the water dropped out of it.

"Do that," he said, "if you have the strength."

"No more than that!" said the Tailor; "why, it's a mere joke to me."

He put his hand into his pocket, and pulling out the bit of soft cheese, he squeezed it till the moisture ran out.

"I guess that will equal you," said he.

The Giant did not know what to say, and could not have believed it of the little man.

Then the Giant picked up a stone, and threw it up so high that one could scarcely follow it with the eye.

3

"Now, then, you sample of a mannikin, do that after me."

"Well thrown!" said the Tailor, "but the stone fell to the ground again. Now I will throw one for you which will never come back again."

So saying, he put his hand into his pocket, took out the bird, and threw it into the air. The bird, rejoiced at its freedom, soared into the air, and was never seen again.

"What do you think of that, Comrade?" asked the Tailor.

"You can certainly throw; but now we will see if you are in a condition to carry anything," said the Giant.

He led the Tailor to a mighty oak which had been felled, and which lay upon the ground.

"If you are strong enough, help me out of the wood with this tree," he said.

"Willingly," answered the little man, "You take the trunk on your shoulder, and I will take the branches; they must certainly be the heaviest."

The Giant accordingly took the trunk on his shoulder; but the Tailor seated himself on one of the branches, and the Giant, who could not look round, had to carry the whole tree, and the Tailor into the bargain. The Tailor was very merry on the end of the tree, and whistled "Three Tailors rode merrily out of the town," as if tree-carrying were a joke to him.

When the Giant had carried the tree some distance, he could go no further, and exclaimed, "Look out, I am going to drop the tree."

The Tailor sprang to the ground with great agility, and seized the tree with both arms, as if he had been carrying it all the time. He said to the Giant: "Big fellow as you are, you can't carry a tree."

After a time they went on together, and when they came to a cherry tree, the Giant seized the top branches, where the cherries ripened first, bent them down, put them in the Tailor's hand, and told him to eat. The Tailor, however, was much too weak to hold the tree, and when the Giant let go, the tree sprang back, carrying the Tailor with it into the air. When he reached the ground again, without any injury, the Giant said, "What's this? Haven't you the strength to hold a feeble sapling?"

"It's not strength that's wanting," answered the Tailor. "Do you think that would be anything to one who killed seven at a blow? I sprang over the tree because some sportsmen were shooting among the bushes. Spring after me if you like."

The Giant made the attempt, but he could not clear the tree, and stuck among the branches. So here, too, the Tailor had the advantage of him.

The Giant said, "If you are such a gallant fellow, come with me to our cave, and stay the night with us."

The Tailor was quite willing, and went with him. When they reached the cave, they found several other Giants sitting round a fire, and each one held a roasted sheep in his hand, which he was eating. The Tailor looked about him, and thought, "It is much more roomy here than in my workshop."

The Giant showed him a bed, and told him to lie down and have a good sleep. The bed was much too big for the Tailor, so he did not lie down in it, but crept into a corner. At midnight, when the Giant thought the Tailor would be in a heavy sleep, he got up, took a big oak club, and with one blow crashed right through the bed, and thought he had put an end to the grasshopper. Early in the morning the Giants went out into the woods, forgetting all about the Tailor, when all at once he appeared before them, as lively as possible. They were terrified, and thinking he would strike them all dead, they ran off as fast as ever they could.

The Tailor went on his way, always following his own pointed nose. When he had walked for a long time, he came to the courtyard of a royal palace. He was so tired that he lay down on the grass and went to sleep. While he lay and slept, the people came and inspected him on all sides, and they read on his belt, "Seven at one blow." "Alas!" they said, "why does this great warrior come here in time of peace; he must be a mighty man."

They went to the King and told him about it; and they were of the opinion that, should war break out, he would be a useful and powerful man, who should on no account be allowed to depart. This advice pleased the King, and he sent one of his courtiers to the Tailor to offer him a military appointment when he woke up. The messenger remained standing by the Tailor, till he opened his eyes and stretched himself, and then he made the offer.

"For that very purpose have I come," said the Tailor. "I am quite ready to enter the King's service."

So he was received with honour, and a special dwelling was assigned to him.

The Soldiers, however, bore him a grudge, and wished him a thousand miles away. "What will be the end of it?" they said to each other. "When we quarrel with him, and he strikes out, seven of us will fall at once. One of us can't cope with him." So they took a resolve, and went altogether to the King, and asked for their discharge. "We are not made," said they, "to hold our own with a man who strikes seven at one blow."

It grieved the King to lose all his faithful servants for the sake of one man; he wished he had never set eyes on the Tailor, and was quite ready to let him go. He did not dare, however, to give him his dismissal, for he was afraid that he would kill him and all his people, and place himself on the throne. He pondered over it for a long time, and at last he thought of a plan. He sent for the Tailor, and said that as he was so great a warrior, he would make him an offer. In a forest in his kingdom lived two Giants, who, by robbery, murder, burning, and laying waste, did much harm. No one dared approach them without being in danger of his life. If he could subdue and kill these two Giants, he would give him his only daughter to be his wife, and half his kingdom as a dowry; also he would give him a hundred Horsemen to accompany and help him.

"That would be something for a man like me," thought the Tailor. "A beautiful Princess and half a kingdom are not offered to one every day." "Oh yes," was his answer, "I will soon subdue the Giants, and that without the hundred Horsemen. He who slays seven at a blow need not fear two." The Tailor set out at once, accompanied by the hundred Horsemen; but when he came to the edge of the forest, he said to his followers, "Wait here, I will soon make an end of the Giants by myself."

Then he disappeared into the wood; he looked about to the right and to the left. Before long he espied both the Giants lying under a tree fast asleep, and snoring. Their snores were so tremendous that they made the branches of the tree dance up and down. The Tailor, who was no fool, filled his pockets with stones, and climbed up the tree. When he got half-way up, he slipped on to a branch just above the sleepers, and then hurled the stones, one after another, on to one of them.

It was some time before the Giant noticed anything; then he woke up, pushed his companion, and said, "What are you hitting me for?"

"You're dreaming," said the other. "I didn't hit you." They went to sleep again, and the Tailor threw a stone at the other one. "What's that?" he cried. "What are you throwing at me?"

"I'm not throwing anything," answered the first one, with a growl.

They quarrelled over it for a time, but as they were sleepy, they made it up, and their eyes closed again.

The Tailor began his game again, picked out his biggest stone, and threw it at the first Giant as hard as he could.

"This is too bad," said the Giant, flying up like a madman. He pushed his companion against the tree with such violence that it shook. The other paid him back in the same coin, and they worked themselves up into such a rage that they tore up trees by the roots, and hacked at each other till they both fell dead upon the ground.

Then the Tailor jumped down from his perch. "It was very lucky," he said, "that they did not tear up the tree I was sitting on, or I should have had to spring on to another like a squirrel, but we are nimble fellows." He drew his sword, and gave each of the Giants two or three cuts in the chest. Then he went out to the Horsemen, and said, "The work is done. I have given both of them the finishing stroke, but it was a difficult job. In their distress they tore trees up by the root to defend themselves; but all that's no good when a man like me comes, who slays seven at a blow."

"Are you not wounded?" then asked the Horsemen.

"There was no danger," answered the Tailor. "Not a hair of my head was touched."

The Horsemen would not believe him, and rode into

the forest to see. There, right enough, lay the Giants in pools of blood, and, round about them, the uprooted trees.

The Tailor now demanded his promised reward from the King; but he, in the meantime, had repented of this promise, and was again trying to think of a plan to shake him off.

"Before I give you my daughter and the half of my kingdom, you must perform one more doughty deed. There is a Unicorn which runs about in the forests doing vast damage; you must capture it."

"I have even less fear of one Unicorn than of two Giants. Seven at one stroke is my style." He took a rope and an axe, and went into the wood, and told his followers to stay outside. He did not have long to wait. The Unicorn soon appeared, and dashed towards the Tailor, as if it meant to run him through with its horn on the spot. "Softly, softly," cried the Tailor. "Not so fast." He stood still, and waited till the animal got quite near, and then he very nimbly dodged behind a tree. The Unicorn rushed at the tree, and ran its horn so hard into the trunk that it had not strength to pull it out again, and so it was caught. "Now I have the prey," said the Tailor, coming from behind the tree. He fastened the rope round the creature's neck, and, with his axe, released the horn from the tree. When this was done he led the animal away, and took it to the King.

Still the King would not give him the promised reward,

but made a third demand of him. Before the marriage, the Tailor must catch a Boar which did much damage in the woods; the Huntsmen were to help him.

"Willingly," said the Tailor. "That will be mere child's play."

He did not take the Huntsmen into the wood with him, at which they were well pleased, for they had already more than once had such a reception from the Boar that they had no wish to encounter him again. When the Boar saw the Tailor, it flew at him with foaming mouth, and, gnashing its teeth, tried to throw him to the ground; but the nimble hero darted into a little chapel which stood near. He jumped out again immediately by the window. The Boar rushed in after the Tailor; but he by this time was hopping about outside, and quickly shut the door upon the Boar. So the raging animal was caught, for it was far too heavy and clumsy to jump out of the window. The Tailor called the Huntsmen up to see the captive with their own eyes.

The hero then went to the King, who was now obliged to keep his word, whether he liked it or not; so he handed over his daughter and half his kingdom to him. Had he known that it was no warrior but only a Tailor who stood before him, he would have taken it even more to heart. The marriage was held with much pomp, but little joy, and a King was made out of a Tailor.

After a time the young Queen heard her husband talking in his sleep, and saying, "Apprentice, bring me the waistcoat, and patch the trousers, or I will break the yard measure over your head." So in this manner she discovered the young gentleman's origin. In the morning she complained to the King, and begged him to rid her of a husband who was nothing more than a Tailor.

The King comforted her, and said, "Tonight, leave your bedroom door open. My servants shall stand outside, and when he is asleep they shall go in and bind him. They shall then carry him away, and put him on board a ship which will take him far away."

The lady was satisfied with this; but the King's armour-bearer, who was attached to his young lord, told him the whole plot.

"I will put a stop to their plan," said the Tailor.

At night he went to bed as usual with his wife. When she thought he was asleep, she got up, opened the door, and went to bed again. The Tailor, who had only pretended to be asleep, began to cry out in a clear voice, "Apprentice, bring me the waistcoat, and you patch the trousers, or I will break the yard measure over your head. I have slain seven at a blow, killed two Giants, led captive a Unicorn, and caught a Boar; should I be afraid of those who are standing outside my chamber door?"

When they heard the Tailor speaking like this, the servants were overcome by fear, and ran away as if wild animals were after them, and none of them would venture near him again.

So the Tailor remained a King till the day of his death.

THE TWELVE DANCING PRINCESSES

THERE was once a King who had twelve daughters, each more beautiful than the other. They slept together in a hall where their beds stood close to one another; and at night, when they had gone to bed, the King fastened the door and bolted it. But when he unlocked it in the morning, he noticed that their shoes had been danced to pieces, and nobody could explain how it happened. So the King sent out a proclamation saying that anyone who could discover where the Princesses did their night's dancing should choose one of them to be his wife and should reign after his death; but whoever presented himself, and failed to make the discovery after three days and nights, was to forfeit his life.

A Prince soon presented himself and offered to take the risk. He was well received, and at night was taken into a room adjoining the hall where the Princesses slept. His bed was made up there, and he was to watch and see where they went to dance; to avoid any secret doings, and to prevent them from going out to any different place, the hall door was left open too. But the eyes of the King's son grew heavy, and he fell asleep. When he woke up in the morning all the twelve had been dancing, for the soles of their shoes were full of holes. The second and third evenings passed with the same results, and then the Prince found no mercy, and his head was cut off. Many others came after him and offered to take the risk, but they all had to lose their lives.

Now it happened that a poor Soldier, who had been wounded and could no longer serve, found himself on the road to the town where the King lived. There he fell in with an old woman who asked him where he intended to go.

"I really don't know myself," he said; and added, in fun, "I should like to discover where the King's daughters dance their shoes into holes, and after that to become King."

"That is not so difficult," said the old woman. "You must not drink the wine which will be brought to you in the evening, but must pretend to be fast asleep." Whereupon she gave him a short cloak, saying: "When you wear this you will be invisible, and then you can slip out after the Twelve Princesses."

As soon as the Soldier heard this good advice he took it up seriously, plucked up courage, appeared before the King, and offered himself as suitor. He was as well received as the others, and was dressed in royal garments.

In the evening, when bed-time came, he was conducted to the ante-room. As he was about to go to bed the eldest Princess appeared, bringing him a cup of wine; but he had fastened a sponge under his chin and let the wine run down into it, so that he did not drink one drop. Then he lay down, and when he had been quiet a little while he began to snore as though in the deepest sleep.

The Twelve Princesses heard him, and laughed. The eldest said: "He, too, must forfeit his life."

Then they got up, opened cupboards, chests, and cases, and brought out their beautiful dresses. They decked themselves before the glass, skipping about and revelling in the prospect of the dance. Only the youngest sister said: "I don't know what it is. You may rejoice, but I feel so strange; a misfortune is certainly hanging over us."

"You are a little goose," answered the eldest; "you are always frightened. Have you forgotten how many Princes have come here in vain? Why, I need not have given the Soldier a sleeping draught at all; the blockhead would never have awakened."

When they were all ready they looked at the Soldier; but his eyes were shut and he did not stir. So they thought they would be quite safe. Then the eldest went up to the bed and knocked on it; it sank into the earth, and they descended through the opening, one after another, the eldest first.

The Soldier, who had noticed everything, did not hesitate long, but threw on his cloak and went down behind the youngest. Half-way down he trod on her dress. She was frightened, and said: "What was that; who is holding on to my dress?"

"Don't be so foolish. You must have caught on a hook,"

said the eldest. Then they went right down, and when they got quite underground, they stood in a marvellously beautiful avenue of trees; all the leaves were silver, and glittered and shone.

The Soldier thought, "I must take away some token with me." He broke off a twig; then a great crash came from the tree.

The youngest cried out, "All is not well; did you hear that sound?"

"Those are triumphant salutes, because we shall soon have released our Princes," said the eldest.

Next they came to an avenue where all the leaves were of gold, and, at last, into a third, where they were of shining diamonds. From both these he broke off a twig, and there was a crack each time which made the youngest Princess start with terror; but the eldest maintained that the sounds were only triumphant salutes. They went on faster, and came to a great lake. Close to the bank lay twelve little boats, and in every boat sat a handsome Prince. They had expected the Twelve Princesses, and each took one with him; but the Soldier seated himself by the youngest.

Then said the Prince, "I don't know why, but the boat is much heavier today, and I am obliged to row with all my strength to get it along."

"I wonder why it is," said the youngest, "unless, perhaps, it is the hot weather; it is strangely hot."

On the opposite side of the lake stood a splendid

brightly-lighted castle, from which came the sound of the joyous music of trumpets and drums. They rowed across, and every Prince danced with his love; and the Soldier danced too, unseen. If one of the Princesses held a cup of wine he drank out of it, so that it was empty when she lifted it to her lips. This frightened the youngest one, but the eldest always silenced her. They danced till three next morning, when their shoes were danced into holes, and they were obliged to stop. The Princes took them back across the lake, and this time the Soldier took his seat beside the eldest. On the bank they said farewell to their Princes, and promised to come again the next night. When they got to the steps, the Soldier ran on ahead, lay down in bed, and when the twelve came lagging by, slowly and wearily, he began to snore again, very loud, so that they said, "We are quite safe as far as he is concerned." Then they took off their beautiful dresses, put them away, placed the worn-out shoes under their beds, and lay down.

The next morning the Soldier determined to say nothing, but to see the wonderful doings again. So he went with them the second and third nights. Everything was just the same as the first time, and they danced each time till their shoes were in holes; but the third time the Soldier took away a wine-cup as a token.

When the appointed hour came for his answer, he took the three twigs and the cup with him and went before the King. The Twelve Princesses stood behind the door listening to hear what he would say. When the King put the question, "Where did my daughters dance their shoes to pieces in the night?" he answered: "With twelve Princes in an underground castle." Then he produced the tokens.

The King sent for his daughters and asked them whether the Soldier had spoken the truth. As they saw that they were betrayed, and would gain nothing by lies, they were obliged to admit all. Thereupon the King asked the Soldier which one he would choose as his wife. He answered: "I am no longer young, give me the eldest."

So the wedding was celebrated that very day, and the kingdom was promised to him on the King's death. But for every night which the Princes had spent in dancing with the Princesses a day was added to their time of enchantment.

HANS IN LUCK

Hans had served his master for seven years, when he one day said to him: "Master, my time is up, I want to go home to my mother; please give me my wages."

His master answered, "You have served me well and faithfully, and as the service has been, so shall the wages be"; and he gave him a lump of gold as big as his head.

Hans took out his pocket-handkerchief and tied up the gold in it, and then slung the bundle over his shoulder, and started on his homeward journey.

As he walked along, just putting one foot before the other, a man on horseback appeared, riding gaily and merrily along on his capering horse.

"Ah!" said Hans, quite loud as he passed, "what a fine thing riding must be. You are as comfortable as if you were in an arm-chair; you don't stumble over any stones; you save your shoes, and you get over the road you hardly know how."

The horseman, who heard him, stopped and said, "Hallo, Hans, why are you on foot?"

"I can't help myself," said Hans, "as I have this bundle to carry home. It is true that it is a lump of gold, but I can hardly hold my head up for it, and it weighs down my shoulder frightfully."

"I'll tell you what," said the horseman, "we will change. I will give you my horse, and you shall give me your bundle."

"With all my heart," said Hans; "but you will be rarely burdened with it."

The horseman dismounted, took the gold, and helped Hans up, put the bridle into his hands, and said: "When you want to go very fast, you must click your tongue and cry 'Gee-up, Gee-up.'"

Hans was delighted when he found himself so easily riding along on horseback. After a time it occurred to him that he might be going faster, and he began to click with his tongue, and to cry "Gee-up, Gee-up." The horse broke into a gallop, and before Hans knew where he was, he was thrown off into a ditch which separated the fields from the high road. The horse would have run away if a peasant coming along the road leading a cow had not caught it. Hans felt himself all over, and picked himself up; but he was very angry, and said to the peasant: "Riding is poor fun at times, when you have a nag like mine, which stumbles and throws you, and puts you in danger of breaking your neck. I will never mount it again. I think much more of your cow there. You can walk comfortably behind her, and you have her milk into the bargain every day, as well as butter and cheese. What would I not give for a cow like that!"

"Well," said the peasant," if you have such a fancy for it as all that, I will exchange the cow for the horse."

Hans accepted the offer with delight, and the peasant mounted the horse and rode rapidly off.

Hans drove his cow peacefully on, and thought what a lucky bargain he had made. "If only I have a bit of bread, and I don't expect ever to be without it, I shall always have butter and cheese to eat with it. If I am thirsty, I only have to milk my cow and I have milk to drink. My heart! what more can you desire?"

When he came to an inn he made a halt, and in his great joy he ate up all the food he had with him, all his dinner and his supper, and he gave the last coins he had for half a glass of beer. Then he went on further in the direction of his mother's village, driving his cow before him. The heat was very oppressive, and, as midday drew near, Hans found himself on a heath which it took him an hour to cross. He was so hot and thirsty, that his tongue was parched and clung to the roof of his mouth.

"This can easily be set to rights," thought Hans. "I will milk my cow and sup up the milk." He tied her to a tree, and as he had no pail, he used his leather cap instead; but, try as hard as he liked, not a single drop of milk appeared. As he was very clumsy in his attempts, the impatient animal gave him a severe kick on his forehead with one of her hind legs. He was stunned by the blow, and fell to the ground, where he lay for some time, not knowing where he was.

Happily just then a butcher came along the road, trundling a young pig in a wheel-barrow.

"What is going on here?" he cried, as he helped poor Hans up.

Hans told him all that had happened.

The butcher handed him his flask, and said: "Here, take a drink, it will do you good. The cow can't give any milk I suppose; she must be too old, and good for nothing but to be a beast of burden, or to go to the butcher."

"Oh dear!" said Hans, smoothing his hair. "Now who would ever have thought it! Killing the animal is all very well, but what kind of meat will it be? For my part, I don't like cow's flesh; it's not juicy enough. Now, if one had a nice young pig like that, it would taste ever so much better; and then, all the sausages!"

"Listen, Hans!" then said the butcher, "for your sake I will exchange, and let you have the pig instead of the cow."

"God reward your friendship!" said Hans, handing over the cow, as the butcher untied the pig, and put the halter with which it was tied into his hand.

Hans went on his way, thinking how well everything was turning out for him. Even if a mishap befell him, something else immediately happened to make up for it. Soon after this, he met a lad carrying a beautiful white goose under his arm. They passed the time of day, and Hans began to tell him how lucky he was, and what successful bargains he had made. The lad told him that he was taking the goose for a christening feast. "Just feel it," he went on, holding it up by the wings. "Feel how heavy

it is; it's true they have been stuffing it for eight weeks. Whoever eats that roast goose will have to wipe the fat off both sides of his mouth."

"Yes, indeed!" answered Hans, weighing it in his hand; "but my pig is no light weight either."

Then the lad looked cautiously about from side to side, and shook his head. "Now, look here," he began, "I don't think it's all quite straight about your pig. One has just been stolen out of Schultze's sty, in the village I have come from. I fear, I fear it is the one you are leading. They have sent people out to look for it, and it would be a bad business for you if you were found with it; the least they would do, would be to put you in the black hole."

Poor Hans was very much frightened at this. "Oh dear! oh dear!" he said. "Do help me out of this trouble. You are more at home here; take my pig, and let me have your goose."

"Well, I shall run some risk if I do, but I won't be the means of getting you into a scrape."

So he took the rope in his hand, and quickly drove the pig up a side road; and honest Hans, relieved of his trouble, plodded on with the goose under his arm.

"When I really come to think it over," he said to himself, "I have still had the best of the bargain. First, there is the delicious roast goose, and then all the fat that will drip out of it in roasting will keep us in goose-fat to eat on our bread for three months at least; and, last of all, there are the beautiful white feathers which I will stuff my pillow with, and then I shall need no rocking to send me to sleep. How delighted my mother will be."

As he passed through the last village he came to a knife-grinder with his cart, singing to his wheel as it buzzed merrily round—

"*Scissors and knives I grind so fast,*
And hang up my cloak against the blast."

Hans stopped to look at him, and at last he spoke to him and said, "You must be doing a good trade to be so merry over your grinding."

"Yes," answered the grinder. "The work of one's hands has a golden foundation. A good grinder finds money whenever he puts his hand into his pocket. But where did you buy that beautiful goose?"

"I did not buy it; I exchanged my pig for it."

"And the pig?"

"Oh, I got that instead of my cow."

"And the cow?"

"I got that for a horse."

"And the horse?"

"I gave a lump of gold as big as my head for it."

"And the gold?"

"Oh, that was my wages for seven years' service."

"You certainly have known how to manage your affairs," said the grinder. "Now, if you could manage to hear the money jingling in your pockets when you got up in the morning, you would indeed have made your fortune."

"How shall I set about that?" asked Hans.

"You must be a grinder like me—nothing is needed for it but a whetstone; everything else will come of itself. I have one here which certainly is a little damaged, but you need not give me anything for it but your goose. Are you willing?"

"How can you ask me such a question?" said Hans. "Why, I shall be the happiest person in the world. If I can have some money every time I put my hand in my pocket, what more should I have to trouble about?"

So he handed him the goose, and took the whetstone in exchange.

"Now," said the grinder, lifting up an ordinary large stone which lay near on the road, "here is another good stone into the bargain. You can hammer out all your old nails on it to straighten them. Take it, and carry it off."

Hans shouldered the stone, and went on his way with a light heart, and his eyes shining with joy. "I must have been born in a lucky hour," he cried; "everything happens just as I want it, and as it would happen to a Sunday's child."

In the meantime, as he had been on foot since daybreak, he began to feel very tired, and he was also very hungry, as he had eaten all his provisions at once, in his joy at his bargain over the cow. At last he could hardly walk any further, and he was obliged to stop every minute to rest. Then the stones were frightfully heavy, and he could not get rid of the thought that it would be very nice if he were not obliged to carry them any further. He dragged himself like a snail to a well in the fields, meaning to rest and refresh himself with a draught of the cool water. So as not to injure the stones by sitting on them, he laid them carefully on the edge of the well. Then he sat down, and was about to stoop down to drink when he inadvertently gave them a little push, and both stones fell straight into the water.

When Hans saw them disappear before his very eyes he jumped for joy, and then knelt down and thanked God, with tears in his eyes, for having shown him this further grace, and relieved him of the heavy stones (which were all that remained to trouble him) without giving him anything to reproach himself with. "There is certainly no one under the sun so happy as I."

And so, with a light heart, free from every care, he now bounded on home to his mother.

THE FROG PRINCE

In the olden time, when wishing was some good, there lived a King whose daughters were all beautiful, but the youngest was so lovely that even the sun, that looked on many things, could not but marvel when he shone upon her face.

Near the King's palace there was a large dark forest, and in the forest, under an old lime-tree, was a well. When the day was very hot the Princess used to go into the forest and sit upon the edge of this cool well; and when she was tired of doing nothing she would play with a golden ball, throwing it up in the air and catching it again, and this was her favourite game. Now on one occasion it so happened that the ball did not fall back into her hand stretched up to catch it, but dropped to the ground and rolled straight into the well. The Princess followed it with her eyes, but it disappeared, and the well was so very deep that it was quite impossible to see the bottom. Then she began to cry bitterly, and nothing would comfort her.

As she was lamenting in this manner, some one called out to her, "What is the matter, Princess? Your lamentations would move the heart of a stone."

She looked round towards the spot whence the voice came, and saw a Toad stretching its broad, ugly face out of the water.

"Oh, it's you, is it, old splasher; I am crying for my golden ball which has fallen into the water."

"Be quiet then, and stop crying," answered the Toad. "I know what to do; but what will you give me if I get you back your plaything?"

"Whatever you like, you dear old Toad," she said. "My clothes, my pearls and diamonds, or even the golden crown upon my head."

The Frog answered, "I care neither for your clothes, your pearls and diamonds, nor even your golden crown; but if you will be fond of me, and let me be your playmate, sit by you at table, eat out of your plate, drink out of your cup, and sleep in your little bed—if you will promise to do all this, I will go down and fetch your ball."

"I will promise anything you like to ask, if only you will get me back my ball."

She thought, "What is the silly old Toad chattering about? He lives in the well, croaking with his mates, and he can't be the companion of a human being."

As soon as the Toad received her promise, he ducked

31

his head under the water and disappeared. After a little while, back he came with the ball in his mouth, and threw it on to the grass beside her.

The Princess was full of joy when she saw her pretty toy again, picked it up, and ran off with it.

"Wait, wait," cried the Toad. "Take me with you; I can't run as fast as you can."

But what was the good of his crying "Croak, croak," as loud as he could? She did not listen to him, but hurried home, and forgot all about the poor Toad; and he had to go back to his well.

The next day, as she was sitting at dinner with the King and all the courtiers, eating out of her golden plate something came flopping up the stairs, flip, flap, flip, flap. When it reached the top it knocked at the door, and cried: "Youngest daughter of the King, you must let me in." She ran to see who it was. When she opened the door and saw the Toad, she shut it again very quickly, and went back to the table, for she was very much frightened.

The King saw that her heart was beating very fast, and he said: "My child, what is the matter? Is there a giant at the door wanting to take you away?"

"Oh no!" she said, "it's not a giant, but a hideous Toad."

"What does the Toad want with you?"

"Oh, father dear, last night, when I was playing by the well in the forest, my golden ball fell into the water. And I cried, and the Toad got it out for me; and then, because he insisted on it, I promised that he should be my playmate. But I never thought that he would come out of the water, but there he is, and he wants to come in to me."

He knocked at the door for the second time, and sang—

> *"Youngest daughter of the King,*
> *Take me up, I sing;*
> *Know'st thou not what yesterday*
> *Thou to me didst say*
> *By the well in forest dell.*
> *Youngest daughter of the King,*
> *Take me up, I sing."*

Then said the King, "What you have promised you must perform. Go and open the door for him."

So she opened the door, and the Toad hobbled in, keeping close to her feet, till he reached her chair. Then he cried, "Lift me up beside you." She hesitated, till the King ordered her to do it. When the Toad was put on the chair, he demanded to be placed upon the table, and then he said, "Push your golden plate nearer that we may eat together." She did as he asked her, but very unwillingly, as could easily be seen. The Toad made a good dinner, but the Princess could not swallow a morsel. At last he said, "I have eaten enough, and I am tired, carry me into your bedroom and arrange your silken bed, that we may go to sleep."

The Princess began to cry, for she was afraid of the clammy Toad, which she did not dare to touch, and which was now to sleep in her pretty little silken bed. But the King grew very angry, and said, "You must not despise anyone who has helped you in your need."

So she seized him with two fingers, and carried him upstairs, where she put him in a corner of her room. When she got into bed, he crept up to her, and said, "I am tired, and I want to go to sleep as well as you. Lift me up, or I will tell your father."

She was very angry, picked him up, and threw him with all her might against the wall, saying, "You may rest there as well as you can, you hideous Toad." When he fell down, he was no longer a hideous Toad, but a handsome Prince with beautiful friendly eyes.

So at her father's wish he became her beloved companion and husband. He told her that he had been bewitched by a wicked fairy, and nobody could have released him from the spells but she herself.

Next morning, when the sun rose, a coach drove up drawn by eight milk-white horses, with white ostrich plumes on their heads, and golden harness. At the back of the carriage stood faithful Henry, the Prince's body-servant. The faithful fellow had been so distressed when his master was changed into a Toad, that he had caused three iron bands to be placed round his heart, lest it should break from grief and pain.

The coach had come to carry the young pair back into the Prince's own kingdom. The faithful Henry lifted both of them into the coach and mounted again behind, delighted at his master's deliverance.

They had only gone a little way when the Prince heard something snapping and cracking behind them. He turned round, and cried—

> *"Henry, the carriage is breaking!"*
> *"No, Sir, that noise I'm a-making,*
> *'Tis the bands round my heart*
> *Just a-coming apart;*
> *For long have you lain,*
> *In trouble and pain,*
> *Like a frog in a well*
> *Fast bound by a spell."*

Once more he heard the same snapping and cracking, and then again. The Prince thought it must be some part of the carriage giving way, but it was only the bands round faithful Henry's heart which were snapping, because of his great joy at his master's deliverance and happiness.

SNOWDROP
(Snow White and the Seven Dwarfs)

IT was the middle of winter, and the snowflakes were falling from the sky like feathers. Now, a Queen sat sewing at a window framed in black ebony, and as she sewed she looked out upon the snow. Suddenly she pricked her finger and three drops of blood fell on to the snow. And the red looked so lovely on the white that she thought to herself: "If only I had a child as white as snow and as red as blood, and as black as the wood of the window frame!" Soon after, she had a daughter, whose hair was black as ebony, while her cheeks were red as blood, and her skin as white as snow; so she was called Snowdrop. But when the child was born the Queen died. A year after the King took another wife. She was a handsome woman, but proud and overbearing, and could not endure that anyone should surpass her in beauty. She had a miraculous looking-glass, and when she stood before it and looked at herself she used to say:

> "Mirror, Mirror on the wall,
> Who is fairest of us all?"

then the Glass answered—

"Queen, thou'rt fairest of them all."

Then she was content, for she knew that the Looking-glass spoke the truth.

But Snowdrop grew up and became more and more beautiful, so that when she was seven years old she was as beautiful as the day, and far surpassed the Queen. Once, when she asked her Glass,

> *"Mirror, Mirror on the wall,*
> *Who is fairest of us all?"*

it answered—

> *"Queen, thee fairest here I hold,*
> *But Snowdrop fairer thousandfold."*

Then the Queen was horror-struck, and turned green and yellow with jealousy. From the hour that she saw Snowdrop her heart sank, and she hated the little girl.

The pride and envy of her heart grew like a weed, so that she had no rest day nor night. At last she called a Huntsman, and said: "Take the child out into the wood and kill her; I will not set eyes on her again."

The Huntsman obeyed, and took Snowdrop out into the forest, but when he drew his hunting-knife and was preparing to plunge it into her innocent heart, she began to cry:

"Alas! dear Huntsman, spare my life, and I will run away into the wild forest and never come back again."

And because of her beauty the Huntsman had pity on her and said, "Well, run away, poor child." Wild beasts will soon devour you, he thought, but still he felt as though a weight were lifted from his heart because he had not been obliged to kill her.

Now the poor child was alone in the great wood, with no living soul near, and she was so frightened that she glanced at all the leaves on the trees and knew not what to do. Then she began to run, and ran over the sharp stones and through the brambles, while the animals passed her by without harming her. She ran as far as her feet could carry her till it was nearly evening; then she saw a little house and went in to rest. Inside, everything was small, but as neat and clean as could be. A small table covered with a white cloth stood ready with seven small plates, and by every plate was a spoon, knife, fork, and cup. Seven little beds were ranged against the walls, covered with snow-white coverlets. As Snowdrop was very hungry and thirsty she ate a little bread and vegetable from each plate, and drank a little wine from each cup, for she did not want to eat up the whole of one portion. Then, being very tired, she lay down in a bed, but none suited her; one was too short, another too long, all except the seventh, which was just right. She remained in it, said her prayers, and fell asleep.

When it was quite dark the masters of the house came in. They were seven Dwarfs, who used to dig in the mountains for ore. They kindled their lights, and as soon as they could see they noticed that someone had been there, for everything was not in the order in which they had left it.

The first said, "Who has been sitting in my chair?"
The second said, "Who has been eating off my plate?"
The third said, "Who has been nibbling my bread?"
The fourth said, "Who has been eating my vegetables?"
The fifth said, "Who has been using my fork?"
The sixth said, "Who has been cutting with my knife?"
The seventh said, "Who has been drinking out of my cup?"

Then the first looked and saw a slight impression on his bed, and said, "Who has been treading on my bed?" The others came running up and said, "And mine, and mine." But the seventh, when he looked into his bed, saw Snowdrop, who lay there asleep. He called the others, who came up and cried out with astonishment, as they held their lights and gazed at Snowdrop. "Heavens! what a beautiful child," they said, and they were so delighted that they did not wake her up but left her asleep in bed. But the seventh dwarf slept with his comrades, an hour with each all through the night.

When morning came Snowdrop woke up, and when she saw the seven Dwarfs she was frightened.

But they were very kind and asked her name.

"I am called Snowdrop," she answered.

"How did you get into our house?" they asked.

Then she told them how her step-mother had wished to get rid of her, how the Huntsman had spared her life, and how she had run all day till she had found the house.

Then the Dwarfs said, "Will you look after our household, cook, make the beds, wash, sew and knit, and keep everything neat and clean? Then you shall stay with us and want for nothing."

"Yes," said Snowdrop, "with all my heart"; and she stayed with them and kept the house in order.

In the morning they went to the mountain and searched for copper and gold, and in the evening they came back and then their meal had to be ready. All day the maiden was alone, and the good Dwarfs warned her and said, "Beware of your step-mother, who will soon learn that you are here. Don't let anyone in."

But the Queen, feeling certain that she was the fairest of all, stepped in front of her Glass, and asked—

> *"Mirror, Mirror on the wall,*
> *Who is fairest of us all?"*

the Glass answered as usual—

> *"Queen, thee fairest here I hold,*
> *But Snowdrop over the fells,*
> *Who with the seven Dwarfs dwells,*
> *Fairer still a thousandfold."*

She was dismayed, for she knew that the Glass told no lies, and she saw that the Hunter had deceived her and that Snowdrop still lived. Accordingly she began to wonder afresh how she might compass her death; for as long as she was not the fairest in the land her jealous heart left her no rest. At last she thought of a plan. She dyed her face and dressed up like an old Pedlar, so that she was quite unrecognizable. In this guise she crossed over the seven mountains to the home of the seven Dwarfs and called out, "Wares for sale."

Snowdrop peeped out of the window and said, "Good-day, mother, what have you got to sell?"

"Good wares, fine wares," she answered, "laces of every colour": and she held out one which was made of gay plaited silk.

"I may let the honest woman in" thought Snowdrop, and she unbolted the door and bought the pretty lace.

"Child," said the Old Woman, "what a sight you are, I will lace you properly for once."

Snowdrop made no objection, and placed herself before the Old Woman to let her lace her with the new lace. But the Old Woman laced so quickly and tightly that she took away Snowdrop's breath and she fell down as though dead.

"Now I am the fairest," she said to herself, and hurried away.

Not long after the seven Dwarfs came home, and were horror-struck when they saw their dear little Snowdrop lying on the floor without stirring, like one dead. When they saw she was laced too tight they cut the lace, where-upon she began to breathe and soon came back to life again. When the Dwarfs heard what had happened, they said that the old Pedlar was no other than the wicked

Queen. "Take care not to let anyone in when we are not here," they said.

Now the wicked Queen, as soon as she got home, went to the Glass and asked—

> *"Mirror, Mirror on the wall,*
> *Who is fairest of us all?"*

and it answered as usual—

> *"Queen, thee fairest here I hold,*
> *But Snowdrop over the fells,*
> *Who with the seven Dwarfs dwells,*
> *Fairer still a thousandfold."*

When she heard it all her blood flew to her heart, so enraged was she, for she knew that Snowdrop had come back to life again. Then she thought to herself, "I must plan something which will put an end to her." By means of witchcraft, in which she was skilled, she made a poisoned comb. Next she disguised herself and took the form of a different Old Woman. She crossed the mountains and came to the home of the seven Dwarfs and knocked at the door calling out, "Good wares to sell."

Snowdrop looked out of the window and said, "Go away, I must not let any one in."

"At least you may look," answered the Old Woman, and she took the poisoned comb and held it up.

The child was so pleased with it that she let herself

be beguiled, and opened the door.

When she had made a bargain the Old Woman said, "Now I will comb your hair properly for once."

Poor Snowdrop, suspecting no evil, let the Old Woman have her way, but scarcely was the poisoned comb fixed in her hair than the poison took effect, and the maiden fell down unconscious.

"You paragon of beauty," said the sinful woman, "now it is all over with you," and she went away.

Happily it was near the time when the seven Dwarfs came home. When they saw Snowdrop lying on the ground as though dead, they immediately suspected her step-mother, and searched till they found the poisoned comb. No sooner had they removed it than Snowdrop came to herself again and related what had happened. They warned her again to be on her guard, and to open the door to no one.

When she got home the Queen stood before her Glass and said—

> "Mirror, Mirror on the wall,
> Who is fairest of us all?"

and it answered as usual—

> "Queen, thee fairest here I hold,
> But Snowdrop over the fells,
> Who with the seven Dwarfs dwells,
> Fairer still a thousandfold."

When she heard the Glass speak these words she trembled and quivered with rage, "Snowdrop shall die," she said, "even if it cost me my own life." Thereupon she went into a secret room, which no one ever entered but herself, and made a poisonous apple. Outwardly it was beautiful to look upon, pale, with rosy cheeks, and everyone who saw it longed for it, but whoever ate of it was certain to die. When the apple was ready she dyed her face and dressed herself like an old Peasant Woman and so crossed the seven hills to the Dwarfs' home. There she knocked.

Snowdrop put her head out of the window and said, "I must not let anyone in, the seven Dwarfs have forbidden me."

"It is all the same to me," said the Peasant Woman. "I shall soon get rid of my apples. There, I will give you one."

"No; I must not take anything."

"Are you afraid of poison?" said the woman. "See, I will cut the apple in half: you eat the red side and I will keep the pale."

Now the apple was so cunningly painted that the red half alone was poisoned. Snowdrop longed for the apple, and when she saw the Peasant Woman eating she could hold out no longer, stretched out her hand and took the poisoned half. Scarcely had she put a bit into her mouth than she fell dead to the ground.

The Queen looked with a fiendish glance, and laughed aloud and said, "White as snow, red as blood, and black as ebony, this time the Dwarfs cannot wake you up again." And when she got home and asked the Looking-glass—

"Mirror, Mirror on the wall,
Who is fairest of us all?"

it answered at last—

"Queen, thou'rt fairest of them all."

Then her jealous heart was at rest, as much at rest as a jealous heart can be. The Dwarfs, when they came at evening, found Snowdrop lying on the ground and not a breath escaped her lips, and she was quite dead. They lifted her up and looked to see whether any poison was to be found, unlaced her dress, combed her hair, washed her with wine and water, but it was no use; their dear child was dead. They laid her on a bier, and all seven sat down and bewailed her and lamented over her for three whole days. Then they prepared to bury her, but she looked so fresh and living, and still had such beautiful rosy cheeks, that they said, "We cannot sink her in the dark earth." And so they had a transparent glass coffin made, so that she could be seen from every side, laid her inside and wrote on it in letters of gold her name and how she was a King's daughter. Then they set the coffin out on the mountain, and one of them always stayed by

her and watched it. And the birds came too and bewailed Snowdrop, first an owl, then a raven, and lastly a dove.

Now Snowdrop lay a long long time in her coffin, looking as though she were asleep. It happened that a Prince was wandering in the wood, and came to the home of the seven Dwarfs to pass the night. He saw the coffin on the mountain and lovely Snowdrop inside, and read what was written in golden letters. Then he said to the Dwarfs, "Let me have the coffin; I will give you whatever you like for it."

But they said, "We will not give it up for all the gold of the world."

Then he said, "Then give it to me as a gift, for I cannot live without Snowdrop to gaze upon; and I will honour and reverence it as my dearest treasure."

When he said these words the good Dwarfs pitied him and gave him the coffin.

The Prince bade his servants carry it on their shoulders. Now it happened that they stumbled over some brushwood, and the shock dislodged the piece of apple from Snowdrop's throat. In a short time she opened her eyes, lifted the lid of the coffin, sat up and came back to life again completely.

"Heavens! where am I?" she asked.

The Prince, full of joy, said, "You are with me," and he related what had happened, and then said, "I love you better than all the world; come with me to my father's castle and be my wife."

Snowdrop agreed and went with him, and their wedding was celebrated with great magnificence. Snowdrop's wicked step-mother was invited to the feast; and when she had put on her fine clothes she stepped to her Glass and asked—

> *"Mirror, Mirror on the wall,*
> *Who is fairest of us all?"*

The Glass answered—

> *"Queen, thee fairest here I hold,*
> *The young Queen fairer thousandfold."*

Then the wicked woman uttered a curse, and was so terribly frightened that she didn't know what to do. Yet she had no rest: she felt obliged to go and see the young Queen. And when she came in and recognised Snowdrop, she choked to death with rage.

Snowdrop and the Prince lived happily for many, many years; and often they went to visit the little Dwarfs who had been so kind to Snowdrop when she needed them.

THE STRAW, THE COAL, AND THE BEAN

ONCE there was a poor old woman who lived in a village; she had collected a bundle of beans, and was going to cook them. So she prepared a fire on her hearth, and to make it burn up quickly she lighted it with a handful of straw. When she threw the beans into the pot, one escaped her unnoticed and slipped on to the floor, where it lay by a straw. Soon after a glowing coal jumped out of the fire and joined the others. Then the Straw began, and said: "Little friends, how came ye hither?"

The Coal answered: "I have happily escaped the fire; and if I had not done so by force of will, my death would certainly have been a most cruel one; I should have been burnt to a cinder."

The Bean said: "I also have escaped so far with a whole skin; but if the old woman had put me into the pot, I should have been pitilessly boiled down to broth like my comrades."

"Would a better fate have befallen me, then?" asked the Straw; "the old woman packed all my brothers into the fire and smoke, sixty of them all done for at once. Fortunately, I slipped through her fingers."

"What are we to do now, though?" asked the Coal.

"My opinion is," said the Bean, "that, as we have escaped death, we must all keep together like good comrades; and so that we may run no further risks, we had better quit the country."

This proposal pleased both the others, and they set out together. Before long they came to a little stream, and, as there was neither path nor bridge, they did not know how to get over. The Straw at last had an idea, and said, "I will throw myself over and then you can walk across upon me like a bridge." So the Straw stretched himself across from one side to the other, and the Coal, which was of a fiery nature, tripped gaily over the newly-built bridge. But when it got to the middle and heard the water rushing below, it was frightened, and remained speechless, not daring to go any further. The Straw beginning to burn, broke in two and fell into the stream; the Coal, falling with it, fizzled out in the water. The Bean, who had cautiously remained on the bank, could not help laughing over the whole business, and, having begun, could not stop, but laughed till she split her sides. Now, all would have been up with her had not, fortunately, a wandering tailor been taking a rest by the stream. As he had a sympathetic heart, he brought out a needle and thread and stitched her up again; but, as he used black thread, all beans have a black seam to this day.

THE FISHERMAN AND HIS WIFE

THERE was once a Fisherman, who lived with his Wife in a miserable little hovel close to the sea. He went to fish every day, and he fished and fished, and at last one day, when he was sitting looking down into the shining water, he felt something on his line. When he hauled it up there was a great Flounder on the end of the line. The Flounder said to him, "Look here, Fisherman, don't kill me; I am no common Flounder. I am an enchanted prince! What good will it do you to kill me? I shan't be good to eat; put me back into the water, and leave me to swim about."

"Well," said the Fisherman, "you need not make so many words about it. I am quite ready to put back a Flounder that can talk." And so saying, he put back the Flounder into the shining water, and it sank down to the bottom, leaving a streak of blood behind it.

Then the Fisherman got up and went back to his Wife in the hovel. "Husband," she said, "hast thou caught nothing today?"

"No," said the Man; "all I caught was one Flounder, and he said he was an enchanted prince, so I let him go swim again."

"Didst thou not wish for anything then?" she asked.

"No," said the Man; "what was there to wish for?"

"Alas!" said his Wife, "isn't it bad enough always to live in this wretched hovel! Thou mightst at least have wished for a nice clean cottage. Go back and call him, tell him I want a pretty cottage: he will surely give us that."

"Alas!" said the Man, "what am I to go back there for?"

"Well," said the Woman, "it was thou who caught him and let him go again; for certain he will do that for thee. Be off now!"

The Man was still not very willing to go, but he did not want to vex his Wife, and at last he went back to the sea.

He found the sea no longer bright and shining, but dull and green. He stood by it and said—

> "Flounder, Flounder in the sea,
>   Prythee, hearken unto me:
>   My Wife, Ilsebil, will have her own way
>   Whatever I will, whatever I say.

The Flounder came swimming up, and said, "Well, what do you want?"

"Alas," said the Man, "I had to call you, for my Wife said I ought to have wished for something as I caught you. She doesn't want to live in our miserable hovel any longer, she wants a pretty cottage."

"Go home again then," said the Flounder, "she has her wish fully."

The Man went home and found his Wife no longer in

the old hut. A pretty cottage stood in its place, and his Wife was sitting on a bench by the door.

She took him by the hand, and said, "Come and look in here—isn't this much better?"

They went inside and found a pretty sittingroom, and a bedroom with a bed in it, a kitchen and a larder furnished with everything of the best in tin and brass and every possible requisite. Outside there was a little yard with chickens and ducks, and a little garden full of vegetables and fruit.

"Look!" said the Woman, "is not this nice?"

"Yes," said the Man, "and so let it remain. We can live here very happily."

"We will see about that," said the Woman. With that they ate dinner and went to bed.

Everything went well for a week or more, and then said the Wife, "Listen, husband, this cottage is too cramped, and the garden is too small. The Flounder could have given us a bigger house. I want to live in a big stone castle. Go to the Flounder, and tell him to give us a castle."

"Alas, Wife!" said the Man, "the cottage is good enough for us. What should we do with a castle?"

"Never mind," said his Wife, "do thou but go to the Flounder, and he will manage it."

"Nay, Wife," said the Man, "the Flounder gave us the cottage. I don't want to go back; as likely as not he'll be angry."

"Go, all the same," said the Woman. "He can do it

easily enough, and willingly into the bargain. Just go!"

The Man's heart was heavy, and he was very unwilling to go. He said to himself, "It's not right." But at last he went.

He found the sea was no longer green; it was still calm, but dark violet and grey. He stood by it and said—

> "Flounder, Flounder in the sea,
> Prythee, hearken unto me:
> My Wife, Ilsebil, will have her own way
> Whatever I will, whatever I say."

"Now, what do you want?" said the Flounder.

"Alas," said the Man, half scared, "my wife wants a big stone castle."

"Go home again," said the Flounder, "she is standing at the door of it."

Then the man went away thinking he would find no house, but when he got back he found a great stone palace, and his Wife standing at the top of the steps, waiting to go in.

She took him by the hand and said, "Come in with me."

With that they went in and found a great hall paved with marble slabs, and numbers of servants in attendance, who opened the great doors for them. The walls were hung with beautiful tapestries, and the rooms were furnished with golden chairs and tables, while rich carpets covered the floors, and crystal chandeliers hung from the ceilings. The tables groaned under every kind of delicate food and the most costly wines. Outside the house there was a great courtyard, with stabling for horses, and cows, and many fine carriages. Beyond this there was a great garden filled with the loveliest flowers, and fine fruit trees. There was also a park, half-a-mile long, and in it were stags and hinds, and hares, and everything of the kind one could wish for.

"Now," said the Woman, "is not this worth having?"

"Oh yes," said the Man; "and so let it remain. We will live in this beautiful palace and be content."

"We will think about that," said his Wife, "and sleep upon it."

With that they went to bed.

Next morning the Wife woke up first. Day was just dawning, and from her bed she could see the beautiful country around her. Her husband was still asleep, but she pushed him with her elbow, and said, "Husband, get up and peep out of the window. See here, now, could we not be King over all this land? Go to the Flounder. We will be King."

"Alas, Wife," said the Man, "what should we be King for? I don't want to be King."

"Ah," said his Wife, "if thou wilt not be King, I will. Go to the Flounder. I will be King."

"Alas, Wife," said the Man, "whatever dost thou want to be King for? I don't like to tell him."

"Why not?" said the Woman. "Go thou must. I will be King."

So the Man went; but he was quite sad because his Wife would be King.

"It is not right," he said; "it is not right."

When he reached the sea, he found it dark, grey, and rough, and evil smelling. He stood there and said—

> *"Flounder, Flounder in the sea,*
> *Prythee, hearken unto me:*
> *My Wife, Ilsebil, will have her own way*
> *Whatever I will, whatever I say."*

"Now, what does she want?" said the Flounder.

"Alas," said the Man, "she wants to be King now."

"Go back. She is King already," said the Flounder.

So the Man went back, and when he reached the palace he found that it had grown much larger, and a great tower had been added with handsome decorations. There was a sentry at the door, and numbers of soldiers were playing drums and trumpets. As soon as he got inside the house, he found everything was marble and gold; and the hangings were of velvet, with great golden tassels. The doors of the saloon were thrown wide open, and he saw the whole court assembled. His Wife was sitting on a lofty throne of gold and diamonds; she wore a golden crown, and carried in one hand a sceptre of pure gold. On each side of her stood her ladies in a long row, every one a head shorter than the next.

He stood before her, and said: "Alas, Wife, art thou now King?"

"Yes," she said; "now I am King."

He stood looking at her for some time, and then he said: "Ah, Wife, it is a fine thing for thee to be King; now we will not wish to be anything more."

"Nay, husband," she answered, "I find that time hangs very heavy on my hands. I can't bear it any longer. Go back to the Flounder. King I am, but I must also be Emperor."

"Alas, Wife," said the Man, "why dost thou now want to be Emperor?"

"Husband," she answered, "go to the Flounder. Emperor I will be."

"Alas, Wife," said the Man, "Emperor he can't make thee, and I won't ask him. There is only one Emperor in the country; and Emperor the Flounder cannot make thee, that he can't."

"What?" said the Woman. "I am King, and thou art but my husband. To him thou must go, and that right quickly. If he can make a King, he can also make an Emperor. Emperor I will be, so quickly go."

He had to go, but he was frightened. And as he went, he thought, "This won't end well; Emperor is too shameless. The Flounder will make an end of the whole thing."

With that he came to the sea, but now he found it quite black, and heaving up from below in great waves. It tossed to and fro, and a sharp wind blew over it, and the man trembled. So he stood there, and said—

> "*Flounder, Flounder in the sea,*
> *Prythee, hearken unto me:*
> *My Wife, Ilsebil, will have her own way*
> *Whatever I will, whatever I say.*"

"What does she want now?" said the Flounder.

"Alas, Flounder," he said, "my Wife wants to be Emperor."

"Go back," said the Flounder. "She is Emperor."

So the man went back, and when he got to the door, he found that the whole palace was made of polished marble, with alabaster figures and golden decorations. Soldiers marched up and down before the doors, blowing their trumpets and beating their drums. Inside the palace, counts, barons, and dukes walked about as attendants, and they opened to him the doors, which were of pure gold.

He went in, and saw his Wife sitting on a huge throne made of solid gold. It was at least two miles high. She had on her head a great golden crown set with diamonds three yards high. In one hand she held the sceptre, and in the other the ball of empire. On each side of her stood the gentlemen-at-arms in two rows, each one a little smaller than the other, from giants two miles high down to the tiniest dwarf no bigger than my little finger. She was surrounded by princes and dukes.

Her husband stood still, and said: "Wife, art thou now Emperor?"

"Yes," said she; "now I am Emperor."

Then he looked at her for some time, and said: "Alas, Wife, how much better off art thou for being Emperor?"

"Husband," she said, "what art thou standing there for? Now I am Emperor, I mean to be Pope! Go back to the Flounder."

"Alas, Wife," said the Man, "what wilt thou not want? Pope thou canst not be. There is only one Pope in Christendom. That's more than the Flounder can do."

"Husband," she said, "Pope I will be; so go at once. I must be Pope this very day."

"No, Wife," he said, "I dare not tell him. It's no good; it's too gross altogether. The Flounder cannot make thee Pope."

"Husband," said the Woman, "don't talk nonsense. If he can make an Emperor, he can make a Pope. Go immediately. I am Emperor, and thou art but my husband, and thou must obey."

So he was frightened, and went; but he was quite dazed. He shivered and shook, and his knees trembled.

A great wind arose over the land, the clouds flew across the sky, and it grew as dark as night; the leaves fell from the trees, and the water foamed and dashed upon the shore. In the distance the ships were being tossed to and fro on the waves, and he heard them firing signals of distress. There was still a little patch of blue in the sky among the dark clouds, but towards the south they were red and heavy, as in a bad storm. In despair, he stood and said—

"Flounder, Flounder in the sea,
Prythee, hearken unto me:
My Wife, Ilsebil, will have her own way
Whatever I will, whatever I say."

"Now, what does she want?" said the Flounder.

"Alas," said the Man, "she wants to be Pope!"

"Go back. Pope she is," said the Flounder.

So back he went, and he found a great church surrounded with palaces. He pressed through the crowd, and inside he found thousands and thousands of lights, and his Wife, entirely clad in gold, was sitting on a still higher throne, with three golden crowns upon her head, and she was surrounded with priestly state. On each side of her were two rows of candles, the biggest as thick as a tower, down to the tiniest little taper. Kings and Emperors were on their knees before her, kissing her shoe.

"Wife," said the Man, looking at her, "art thou now Pope?"

"Yes," said she; "now I am Pope."

So there he stood gazing at her, and it was like looking at a shining sun.

"Alas, Wife," he said, "art thou better off for being Pope?" At first she sat as stiff as a post, without stirring. Then he said: "Now, Wife, be content with being Pope; higher thou canst not go."

"I will think about that," said the Woman, and with that they both went to bed. Still she was not content, and could hardly sleep for her inordinate desires. The Man slept well and soundly, for he had walked about a great deal in the day; but his Wife could think of nothing but what further grandeur she could demand. When the dawn reddened the sky, she raised herself up in bed and looked out of the window, and when she saw the sun rise, she said:

"Ha! can I not cause the sun and the moon to rise? Husband!" she cried, digging her elbow into his side, "wake up and go to the Flounder. I will be Lord of the Universe."

Her husband, who was still more than half asleep, was so shocked that he fell out of bed. He thought he must have heard wrong. He rubbed his eyes, and said:

"Alas, Wife, what didst thou say?"

"Husband," she said, "if I cannot be Lord of the Universe, and cause the sun and the moon to set and rise, I shall not be able to bear it. I shall never have another happy moment."

She looked at him so wildly that it caused a shudder to run through him.

"Alas, Wife," he said, falling on his knees before her, "the Flounder can't do that. Emperor and Pope he can make, but that is indeed beyond him. I pray thee, control thyself and remain Pope."

Then she flew into a terrible rage. Her hair stood on end; she kicked him and screamed—

"I won't bear it any longer; wilt thou go!"

Then he pulled on his trousers and tore away like a

madman. Such a storm was raging that he could hardly keep his feet: houses and trees quivered and swayed, and mountains trembled, and the rocks rolled into the sea. The sky was pitchy black; it thundered and lightened, and the sea ran in black waves mountains high, crested with white foam. He shrieked out, but could hardly make himself heard—

> *"Flounder, Flounder in the sea,*
> *Prythee, hearken unto me:*
> *My Wife, Ilsebil, will have her own way*
> *Whatever I will, whatever I say."*

"Now, what does she want?" asked the Flounder.

"Alas," he said, "she wants to be Lord of the Universe."

"Now she must go back to her old hovel; and there she is."

So there they are to this very day.

THE CAT AND MOUSE
IN PARTNERSHIP

A CAT once made the acquaintance of a Mouse, and she
said so much to it about her love and friendship that at
last the Mouse agreed to go into partnership and live
together with her.

"We must take precautions for the winter," said the
Cat, "or we shall suffer from hunger. You, little Mouse,
dare not venture everywhere, and in the end you will get
me into a scrape."

So the good advice was followed, and a pot of fat
was purchased. They did not know where to keep it,
but, after much deliberation, the Cat said, "I know no
place where it would be safer than in the church; nobody
dare venture to take anything there. We will put it under

the altar, and will not touch it till we are obliged to."

So the pot was deposited in safety; but, before long, the Cat began to hanker after it, and said to the Mouse:

"Oh, little Mouse, my cousin has asked me to be god-mother. She has brought a son into the world. He is white, with brown spots; and I am to hold him at the font. Let me go out today, and you stay alone to look after the house."

"Oh yes," said the Mouse, "for goodness sake, go; and if you have anything nice to eat, think of me. I would gladly have a drop of sweet raspberry wine myself."

Now there wasn't a word of truth in all this. The Cat had no cousin, and she had not been invited to be god-mother at all. She went straight to the church, crept to the pot of fat, and began to lick it, and she licked and licked the whole of the top off it. Then she took a stroll on the house-tops and reflected on her proceedings, after which she stretched herself in the sun, and wiped her whiskers every time she thought of the pot of fat. She did not go home till evening.

"Oh, there you are again," said the Mouse; "you must have had a merry time."

"Oh, well enough," answered the Cat.

"What kind of name was given to the child?" asked the Mouse.

"Top-off," answered the Cat, drily.

"Top-off!" cried the Mouse. "What an extraordinary name; is it a common one in your family?"

"What does it matter?" said the Cat. "It's not worse than crumbstealers, as your godchildren are called."

Not long after the Cat was again overcome by her desires. She said to the Mouse, "You must oblige me again by looking after the house alone. For the second time, I have been asked to be sponsor, and, as the child has a white ring round its neck, I can't refuse."

The good little Mouse was quite ready to oblige, and the Cat stole away behind the city walls to the church, and ate half of the pot of fat. "Nothing tastes better," she said, "than what one eats by oneself"; and she was quite satisfied with her day's work. When she got home, the Mouse asked what this child had been named.

"Half-gone."

"What do you say? I have never heard such a name in my life. I don't believe you would find it in the calendar."

Soon the Cat's mouth watered again for the dainty morsel.

"Good things always come in threes," she said to the Mouse; "again I am to stand sponsor. This child is quite black, with big white paws, but not another white hair on its body. Such a thing only occurs once in a few years. You will let me go out again, won't you?"

"Top-off! Half-gone! They are such curious names; they set me thinking."

"You sit at home in your dark velvet coat," said the Cat, "getting your head full of fancies. It all comes of not going out in the daytime."

During the Cat's absence, the Mouse cleared up and made the house tidy; but the greedy Cat ate up all the fat. "When it's all gone, one can be at peace," said she to herself, as she went home, late at night, fat and satiated.

The Mouse immediately asked what name had been given to the third child.

"I don't suppose it will please you any better," said the Cat. "He is called All-gone!"

"All-gone!" exclaimed the Mouse. "I have never seen it in print, All-gone! What is the meaning of it?"

She shook her head, rolled herself up, and went to sleep.

From this time nobody asked the Cat to be sponsor. But when the winter came, and it grew very difficult to get food, the Mouse remembered their store, and said, "Come, Cat, we will go to our pot of fat which we have saved up; won't it be good now?"

"Yes, indeed!" answered the Cat; "it will do you just as much good as putting your tongue out of the window."

They started off to the church, and when they got there, they found the fat-pot still in its place, but it was quite empty.

"Alas," said the mouse, "now I see it all. Everything has come to the light of day. You have indeed been a true friend! You ate it all up when you went to be godmother. First Top-off, then Half-gone, then——"

"Hold your tongue," cried the Cat. "Another word,

and I'll eat you too."

The unfortunate Mouse had "All-gone" on its lips, but hardly had it come out than the Cat made a spring, seized the Mouse, and gobbled it up.

Now, that's the way of the world, you see.

DOCTOR KNOW-ALL

ONCE upon a time a poor Peasant, named Crabb, was taking a load of wood drawn by two oxen to the town for sale. He sold it to a Doctor for two dollars. When the money was being paid to him, it so happened that the Doctor was sitting at dinner. When the Peasant saw how daintily the Doctor was eating and drinking, he felt a great desire to become a Doctor too. He remained standing and looking on for a time, and then asked if he could not be a Doctor.

"Oh yes!" said the Doctor; "that is easily managed."

"What must I do?" asked the Peasant.

"First buy an ABC book; you can get one with a cock as a frontispiece. Secondly, turn your wagon and oxen into money, and buy with it clothes and other things suitable for a Doctor. Thirdly, have a sign painted with the words, 'I am Doctor Know-All,' and have it nailed over your door."

The Peasant did everything that he was told to do. Now when he had been doctoring for a while, not very long though, a rich nobleman had some money stolen from him. He was told about Doctor Know-All, who lived in such and such a village, who would be sure to know what had become of it. So the gentleman ordered his carriage and drove to the village.

He stopped at the Doctor's house, and asked Crabb if he were Doctor Know-All.

"Yes, I am."

"Then you must go with me to get my stolen money back."

"Yes, certainly; but Grethe, my wife, must come too."

The nobleman agreed, and gave both of them seats in his carriage, and they all drove off together.

When they reached the nobleman's castle the dinner was ready, and Crabb was invited to sit down to table.

"Yes; but Grethe, my wife, must dine too"; and he seated himself with her.

When the first Servant brought in a dish of choice

food, the Peasant nudged his wife, and said: "Grethe, that was the first,"—meaning that the servant was handing the first dish. But the servant thought he meant to say, "That was the first thief." As he really was the thief, he became much alarmed, and said to his comrades outside—

"That Doctor knows everything, we shan't get out of this hole; he said I was the first."

The second Servant did not want to go in at all, but he had to go, and when he offered his dish to the Peasant, he nudged his wife, and said—"Grethe, that is the second."

This Servant was also frightened and hurried out.

The third one fared no better. The Peasant said again: "Grethe, that is the third."

The fourth one brought in a covered dish, and the master told the Doctor that he must show his powers and guess what was under the cover. Now it was a dish of crabs.

The Peasant looked at the dish and did not know what to do, so he said: "Wretched Crabb that I am."

When the Master heard him he cried: "There, he knows it! Then he knows where the money is too."

Then the Servant grew terribly frightened, and signed to the Doctor to come outside.

When he went out, they all four confessed to him that they had stolen the money; they would gladly give it to him and a large sum in addition, if only he would not betray them to their Master, or their necks would be in peril. They also showed him where the money was hidden. Then the Doctor was satisfied, went back to the table, and said—

"Now, Sir, I will look in my book to see where the money is hidden."

The fifth, in the meantime, had crept into the stove to hear if the Doctor knew still more. But he sat there turning over the pages of his ABC book looking for the cock, and as he could not find it at once, he said: "I know you are there, and out you must come."

The man in the stove thought it was meant for him, and sprang out in a fright, crying: "The man knows everything."

Then Doctor Know-All showed the nobleman where the money was hidden, but he did not betray the servants; and he received much money from both sides as a reward, and became a very celebrated man.

THE BREMEN TOWN-MUSICIANS

ONCE upon a time a man had an Ass which for many years carried sacks to the mill indefatigably. At last, however, its strength was worn out; it was no longer of any use for work. Accordingly its master began to ponder as to how best to cut down its keep; but the Ass, observing that there was mischief in the air, ran away and started on the road to Bremen; there he thought he could become a town-musician.

When he had been travelling a short time, he fell in with a hound, who was lying panting on the road as though he had run himself off his legs.

"Well, what are you panting for, Packan?" said the Ass.

"Ah," said the Dog, "just because I am old, and every day I get weaker, and also because I can no longer keep up with the pack, my master wanted to kill me, so I took my departure. But now, how am I to earn my bread?"

"Do you know what," said the Ass, "I am going to Bremen, and shall there become a town-musician; come with me and take your part in the music. I shall play the lute, and you shall beat the kettle-drum."

The Dog agreed, and they went on.

A short time after they came upon a Cat, sitting in the road, with a face as long as a wet week.

"Well, what has been crossing you, Whiskers?" asked the Ass.

"Who can be cheerful when he is out at elbows?" said the Cat. "I am getting on in years, and my teeth are blunted, and I prefer to sit by the stove and purr instead of hunting round after mice. Just because of this my mistress wanted to drown me. I made myself scarce, but the situation is very critical."

"Come with us to Bremen," said the Ass. "You are a great hand at serenading, so you can become a town-musician."

The Cat consented, and joined them.

Next the fugitives passed by a yard where a barn-door fowl was sitting on the floor, crowing with all its might.

"You crow so loud you pierce one through and through," said the Ass. "What is the matter?"

"Why! didn't I prophesy fine weather for Lady Day, when Our Lady washes the Christ Child's little garment and wants to dry it? But, notwithstanding this, because Sunday visitors are coming tomorrow, the mistress has no pity, and she has ordered the cook to make me into soup, so I shall have my neck wrung tonight. Now I am crowing with all my might while I have the chance."

"Come along, Red-comb," said the Ass; "you had much better come with us. We are going to Bremen, and you will find a much better fate there. You have a good voice, and when we make music together, there will be quality in it."

The Cock allowed himself to be persuaded, and they all four went off together. They could not, however, reach the town in one day, and by evening they arrived at a wood, where they determined to spend the night. The Ass and the Dog lay down under a big tree; the Cat and the Cock settled themselves in the branches, the Cock flying right up to the top, which was the safest place for him. Before going to sleep he looked round once more in every direction; suddenly it seemed to him that he saw a light burning in the distance. He called out to his comrades that there must be a house not far off, for he saw a light.

"Very well," said the Ass, "let us set out and make our way to it, for the entertainment here is very bad."

The Dog thought some bones or meat would suit him too, so they set out in the direction of the light, and soon saw it shining more clearly, and getting bigger and bigger, till they reached a brightly-lighted robber's den. The Ass, being the tallest, approached the window and looked in.

"What do you see, old moke?" asked the Cock.

"What do I see?" answered the Ass; "why, a table spread with delicious food and drink, and robbers seated at it enjoying themselves."

"That would just suit us," said the Cock.

"Yes; if we were only there," answered the Ass.

Then the animals took counsel as to how to set about driving the robbers out. At last they hit upon a plan.

The Ass was to take up his position with his fore-feet on the window-sill, the Dog was to jump on his back, the Cat was to climb up on to the Dog, and last of all the Cock flew up and perched on the Cat's head. When they were thus arranged, at a given signal they all began to perform their music; the Ass brayed, the Dog barked, the Cat mewed, and the Cock crowed; then they dashed through the window, shivering the panes. The robbers jumped up at the terrible noise; they thought nothing less than a demon was coming in upon them, and fled into the wood in the greatest alarm. Then the four animals sat down to table, and helped themselves according to taste, and ate as though they had been starving for weeks. When they had finished they extinguished the light, and looked for sleeping places, each one to suit his nature and taste.

The Ass lay down on the manure heap, the Dog behind the door, the Cat on the hearth near the warm ashes, and the Cock flew up to the rafters. As they were tired from the long journey, they soon went to sleep.

When midnight was past, and the robbers saw from a distance that the light was no longer burning, and that all seemed quiet, the chief said:

"We ought not to have been scared by a false alarm," and ordered one of the robbers to go and examine the house.

Finding all quiet, the messenger went into the kitchen to kindle a light, and taking the Cat's glowing, fiery eyes for live coals, he held a match close to them so as to light it. But the Cat would stand no nonsense; it flew at his face, spat and scratched. He was terribly frightened and ran away.

He tried to get out by the back door, but the Dog, who was lying there, jumped up and bit his leg. As he ran across the manure heap in front of the house, the Ass gave him a good sound kick with his hind legs, while the Cock, who had awoken at the uproar quite fresh and gay, cried out from his perch: "Cock-a-doodle-doo." Thereupon the robber ran back as fast as he could to his chief, and said: "There is a gruesome witch in the house, who breathed on me and scratched me with her long fingers. Behind the door there stands a man with a knife, who stabbed me; while in the yard lies a black monster, who hit me with a club; and upon the roof the judge is seated, and he called out, 'Bring the rogue here,' so I hurried away as fast as I could."

Thenceforth the robbers did not venture again to the house, which, however, pleased the four Bremen musicians so much that they never wished to leave it again.

ASHENPUTTEL
(Cinderella)

THE wife of a rich man fell ill, and when she felt that she was nearing her end, she called her only daughter to her bedside, and said:

"Dear child, continue devout and good, then God will always help you, and I will look down upon you from heaven, and watch over you."

Thereupon she closed her eyes, and breathed her last.

The maiden went to her mother's grave every day and wept, and she continued to be devout and good. When the winter came, the snow spread a white covering on the grave, and when the sun of spring had unveiled it again, the husband took another wife. The new wife brought home with her two daughters, who were fair and beautiful to look upon, but base and black at heart.

Then began a sorry time for the unfortunate step-child.

"Is this stupid goose to sit with us in the parlour?" they said.

"Whoever wants to eat bread must earn it; go and sit with the kitchenmaid."

They took away her pretty clothes, and made her put on an old grey frock, and gave her wooden clogs.

"Just look at the proud Princess, how well she's

dressed," they cried, as, laughing, they led her to the kitchen. There, the girl was obliged to do hard work from morning till night, to get up at daybreak, carry water, light the fire, cook, and wash. Not content with that, the sisters inflicted on her every conceivable vexation; they made fun of her, and tossed the peas and lentils among the ashes, so that she had to sit down and pick them out again. In the evening, when she was worn out with work, she had no bed to go to, but had to lie on the hearth among the cinders. And because, on account of that, she always looked dusty and dirty, they called her Ashenputtel.

It happened one day that the Father had a mind to go to the Fair. So he asked both his step-daughters what he should bring home for them.

"Fine clothes," said one.

"Pearls and jewels," said the other.

"But you, Ashenputtel?" said he, "what will you have?"

"Father, break off for me the first twig which brushes against your hat on your way home."

Well, he brought home for his two step-daughters beautiful clothes, pearls and jewels, and on his way home, as he was riding through a green copse, a hazel twig grazed him and knocked his hat off. Then he broke off the branch and took it with him.

When he got home he gave his step-daughters what they had asked for, and to Ashenputtel he gave the twig from the hazel bush.

Ashenputtel thanked him, and went to her mother's grave and planted the twig upon it; she wept so much that her tears fell down and watered it. However, it grew and became a fine tree.

Ashenputtel went down to the grave three times every day, wept and prayed, and every time a little white bird came and perched upon the tree, and when she uttered a wish, the little bird threw down to her what she had wished for.

Now it happened that the King proclaimed a festival, which was to last three days, and to which all the beautiful maidens in the country were invited, in order that his son might choose a bride.

When the two step-daughters heard that they were also to be present, they were in high spirits, called Ashenputtel, and said:

"Brush our hair and clean our shoes, and fasten our buckles, for we are going to the feast at the King's palace."

Ashenputtel obeyed, but wept, for she also would gladly have gone to the ball with them, and begged her Step-mother to give her leave to go.

"You, Ashenputtel!" she said. "Why, you are covered with dust and dirt. You go to the festival! Besides, you have no clothes nor shoes, and yet you want to go to the ball."

As she, however, continued asking, her Step-mother said:

"Well, I have thrown a dishful of lentils into the cinders, if you have picked them all out in two hours you shall go with us."

The girl went through the back door into the garden, and cried, "Ye gentle doves, ye turtle doves, and all ye little birds under heaven, come and help me,

> *"The good into a dish to throw,*
> *The bad into your crops can go."*

Then two white doves came in by the kitchen window, and were followed by the turtle doves, and finally all the little birds under heaven flocked in, chirping, and settled down among the ashes. And the doves gave a nod with their little heads, peck, peck, peck; and then the rest began also, peck, peck, peck, and collected all the good beans into the dish. Scarcely had an hour passed before they had finished, and all flown out again.

Then the girl brought the dish to her Step-mother, and was delighted to think that now she would be able to go to the feast with them.

But she said, "No, Ashenputtel, you have no clothes, and cannot dance; you will only be laughed at."

But when she began to cry, the Step-mother said:

"If you can pick out two whole dishes of lentils from the ashes in an hour, you shall go with us."

And she thought, "She will never be able to do that."

When her Step-mother had thrown the dishes of lentils

among the ashes, the girl went out through the back door, and cried, "Ye gentle doves, ye turtle doves, and all ye little birds under heaven, come and help me,

> *"The good into a dish to throw,*
> *The bad into your crops can go."*

Then two white doves came in by the kitchen window, and were followed by the turtle doves, and all the other little birds under heaven, and in less than an hour the whole had been picked up, and they had all flown away.

Then the girl carried the dish to her Step-mother, and was delighted to think that she would now be able to go to the ball.

But she said, "It's not a bit of good. You can't go with us, for you've got no clothes, and you can't dance. We should be quite ashamed of you."

Thereupon she turned her back upon her, and hurried off with her two proud daughters.

As soon as everyone had left the house, Ashenputtel went out to her mother's grave under the hazel-tree, and cried:

> *"Shiver and shake, dear little tree,*
> *Gold and silver shower on me."*

Then the bird threw down to her a gold and silver robe, and a pair of slippers embroidered with silk and silver. With all speed she put on the robe and went to the feast.

But her step-sisters and their mother did not recognize her, and supposed that she was some foreign Princess, so beautiful did she appear in her golden dress. They never gave a thought to Ashenputtel, but imagined that she was sitting at home in the dirt picking the lentils out of the cinders.

The Prince came up to the stranger, took her by the hand, and danced with her. In fact, he would not dance with anyone else, and never let go of her hand. If anyone came up to ask her to dance, he said, "This is my partner."

She danced until nightfall, and then wanted to go home; but the Prince said, "I will go with you and escort you."

For he wanted to see to whom the beautiful maiden belonged. But she slipped out of his way and sprang into the pigeon-house.

Then the Prince waited till her Father came, and told him that the unknown maiden had vanished into the pigeon-house.

The old man thought, "Could it be Ashenputtel?" And he had an axe brought to him, so that he might break down the pigeon-house, but there was no one inside.

When they went home, there lay Ashenputtel in her dirty clothes among the cinders, and a dismal oil lamp was burning in the chimney. For Ashenputtel had quietly jumped down out of the pigeon-house and run back to the hazel-tree. There she had taken off her beautiful clothes and laid them on the grave, and the bird had taken them away again. Then she had settled herself among the ashes on the hearth in her old grey frock.

On the second day, when the festival was renewed, and her parents and step-sisters had started forth again, Ashenputtel went to the hazel-tree, and said:

"Shiver and shake, dear little tree,
Gold and silver shower on me."

Then the bird threw down a still more gorgeous robe than on the previous day. And when she appeared at the festival in this robe, everyone was astounded by her beauty.

But the King's son had waited till she came, and at once took her hand, and she danced with no one but him. When others came forward and invited her to dance, he said, "This is my partner."

At nightfall she wished to leave; but the Prince went after her, hoping to see into what house she went, but she sprang out into the garden behind the house. There stood a fine big tree on which the most delicious pears hung. She climbed among the branches as nimbly as a squirrel, and the Prince could not make out what had become of her.

But he waited till her Father came, and then said to him, "The unknown maiden has slipped away from me, and I think that she jumped into the pear-tree."

The Father thought, "Can it be Ashenputtel?" And he had the axe brought to cut down the tree, but there was no one on it. When they went home and looked into the kitchen, there lay Ashenputtel among the cinders as usual; for she had jumped down on the other side of the tree, taken back the beautiful clothes to the bird on the hazel-tree, and put on her old grey frock.

On the third day, when her parents and sisters had started, Ashenputtel went again to her mother's grave, and said:

> *"Shiver and shake, dear little tree,*
> *Gold and silver shower on me."*

Then the bird threw down a dress which was so magnificent that no one had ever seen the like before, and the slippers were entirely of gold. When she appeared at the festival in this attire, they were all speechless with astonishment. The Prince danced only with her, and if anyone else asked her to dance, he said, "This is my partner."

When night fell and she wanted to leave, the Prince was more desirous than ever to accompany her, but she darted away from him so quickly that he could not keep up with her. But the Prince had used a stratagem, and had caused the steps to be covered with cobbler's wax. The consequence was, that as the maiden sprang down them, her left slipper remained sticking there. The Prince took it up. It was small and dainty, and entirely made of gold.

The next morning he went with it to Ashenputtel's Father, and said to him, "No other shall become my wife but she whose foot this golden slipper fits."

The two sisters were delighted thereat, for they both had beautiful feet. The eldest went into the room intending to try on the slipper, and her Mother stood beside her. But her great toe prevented her getting it on, her foot was too long.

The girl cut off her toe, forced her foot into the slipper, stifled her pain, and went out to the Prince. Then he took her up on his horse as his Bride, and rode away with her.

However, they had to pass the grave on the way, and there sat the two Doves on the hazel-tree, and cried:

> "Prithee, look back, prithee, look back,
>   There's blood on the track,
>   The shoe is too small,
>   The true Bride at home waits thy call."

Then he looked at her foot and saw how the blood was streaming from it. So he turned his horse round and carried the false Bride back to her home, and said that she was not the right one; the second sister must try the shoe.

Then she went into the room, and succeeded in getting her toes into the shoe, but her heel was too big.

The maiden cut a bit off her heel, forced her foot into the shoe, stifled her pain, and went out to the Prince.

Then he took her up on his horse as his Bride, and rode off with her.

As they passed the grave, the two Doves were sitting on the hazel-tree, and crying:

> *"Prithee, look back, prithee, look back,*
> *There's blood on the track,*
> *The shoe is too small,*
> *The true Bride at home waits thy call."*

He looked down at her foot and saw that it was streaming with blood, and there were deep red spots on her stockings. Then he turned his horse and brought the false Bride back to her home.

"This is not the right one either," he said. "Have you no other daughter?"

"No," said the man. "There is only a daughter of my late wife's, a puny, stunted drudge, but she cannot possibly be the Bride."

The Prince said that she must be sent for.

But the Mother answered, "Oh no, she is much too dirty; she mustn't be seen on any account."

He was, however, absolutely determined to have his way, and they were obliged to summon Ashenputtel.

When she had washed her hands and face, she went up and curtsied to the Prince, who handed her the golden slipper.

Then she sat down on a bench, pulled off her wooden clog and put on the slipper, which fitted to a nicety.

And when she stood up and the Prince looked into her face, he recognised the beautiful maiden that he had danced with, and cried: "This is the true Bride!"

The Step-mother and the two sisters were dismayed and turned white with rage; but he took Ashenputtel on his horse and rode off with her.

As they rode past the hazel-tree the two White Doves cried:

> *"Prithee, look back, prithee, look back,*
> *No blood's on the track,*
> *The shoe's not too small,*
> *You carry the true Bride home to your hall."*

RAPUNZEL

THERE was once a man and his wife who had long wished in vain for a child, when at last they had reason to hope that Heaven would grant their wish. There was a little window at the back of their house, which overlooked a beautiful garden, full of lovely flowers and shrubs. It was, however, surrounded by a high wall, and nobody dared to enter it, because it belonged to a powerful Witch, who was feared by everybody.

One day the woman, standing at this window and looking into the garden, saw a bed planted with beautiful corn-salad. It looked so fresh and green that it made her long to eat some of it. This longing increased every day, and as she knew it could never be satisfied, she began to look pale and miserable, and to pine away. Then her husband was alarmed, and said: "What ails you, my dear wife?"

"Alas!" she answered, "if I cannot get any of the corn-salad from the garden behind our house to eat, I shall die."

Her husband, who loved her, thought, "Before you let your wife die, you must fetch her some of that corn-salad, cost what it may." So in the twilight he climbed over the

wall into the Witch's garden, hastily picked a handful of corn-salad, and took it back to his wife. She immediately dressed it, and ate it up very eagerly. It was so very, very nice, that the next day her longing for it increased three-fold. She could have no peace unless her husband fetched her some more. So in the twilight he set out again; but when he got over the wall he was terrified to see the Witch before him.

"How dare you come into my garden like a thief, and steal my corn-salad?" she said, with angry looks. "It shall disagree with you."

"Alas!" he answered, "be merciful to me; I am only here from necessity. My wife sees your corn-salad from the window, and she has such a longing for it, that she would die if she could not get some of it."

The anger of the Witch abated, and she said to him, "If it is as you say, I will allow you to take away with you as much corn-salad as you like, but on one condition. You must give me the child which your wife is about to bring into the world. I will care for it like a mother, and all will be well with it." In his fear the man consented to everything, and when the baby was born, the Witch appeared, gave it the name of Rapunzel (corn-salad), and took it away with her.

Rapunzel was the most beautiful child under the sun. When she was twelve years old, the Witch shut her up in a tower which stood in a wood. It had neither staircase nor doors, and only a little window quite high up in the wall. When the Witch wanted to enter the tower, she stood at the foot of it, and cried—

"Rapunzel, Rapunzel, let down your hair."

Rapunzel had splendid long hair, as fine as spun gold. As soon as she heard the voice of the Witch, she unfastened her plaits and twisted them round a hook by the window. They fell twenty ells downwards, and the Witch climbed up by them.

It happened a couple of years later that the King's son rode through the forest, and came close to the tower. From thence he heard a song so lovely, that he stopped to listen. It was Rapunzel, who in her loneliness made her sweet voice resound to pass away the time. The King's son wanted to join her, and he sought for the door of the tower, but there was none to find.

He rode home, but the song had touched his heart so deeply that he went into the forest every day to listen to it. Once, when he was hidden behind a tree, he saw a Witch come to the tower and call out—

"Rapunzel, Rapunzel, let down your hair."

Then Rapunzel lowered her plaits of hair and the Witch climbed up to her.

"If that is the ladder by which one ascends, I will try my luck myself." And the next day, when it began to grow dark, he went to the tower and cried—

"Rapunzel, Rapunzel, let down your hair."

The hair fell down at once, and the King's son climbed up by it.

At first Rapunzel was terrified, for she had never set eyes on a man before, but the King's son talked to her in a friendly way, and told her that his heart had been so deeply touched by her song that he had no peace, and he was obliged to see her. Then Rapunzel lost her fear, and when he asked if she would have him for her husband, and she saw that he was young and handsome, she thought, "He will love me better than old Mother Gothel." So she said, "Yes," and laid her hand in his. She said "I will gladly go with you, but I do not know how I am to get down from this tower. When you come, will you bring a skein of silk with you every time. I will twist it into a ladder, and when it is long enough I will descend by it, and you can take me away with you on your horse."

She arranged with him that he should come and see her every evening, for the old Witch came in the daytime.

The Witch discovered nothing, till suddenly Rapunzel said to her, "Tell me, Mother Gothel, how can it be that you are so much heavier to draw up than the young Prince who will be here in a moment?"

"Oh, you wicked child, what do you say? I thought I had separated you from all the world, and yet you have deceived me." In her rage she seized Rapunzel's beautiful hair, twisted it twice round her left hand, snatched up a pair of shears and cut off the plaits, which fell to the ground. She was so merciless that she took poor Rapunzel away into a wilderness, where she forced her to live in the greatest grief and misery.

In the evening of the day on which she had banished Rapunzel, the Witch fastened the plaits which she had cut off to the hook by the window, and when the Prince came and called—

"Rapunzel, Rapunzel, let down your hair,"
she lowered the hair. The Prince climbed up, but there he found, not his beloved Rapunzel, but the Witch, who looked at him with angry and wicked eyes.

"Ah!" she cried mockingly, "you have come to fetch your lady love, but the pretty bird is no longer in her nest; and she can sing no more, for the cat has seized her, and it will scratch your own eyes out too. Rapunzel is lost to you; you will never see her again."

The Prince was beside himself with grief, and in his despair he sprang out of the window. He was not killed, but his eyes were scratched out by the thorns among which he fell. He wandered about blind in the wood, and had nothing but roots and berries to eat. He did nothing but weep and lament over the loss of his beloved Rapunzel. In this way he wandered about for some years, till at last he reached the wilderness where Rapunzel had been living in great poverty.

He heard a voice which seemed very familiar to him, and he went towards it. Rapunzel knew him at once, and fell weeping upon his neck. Two of her tears fell upon his eyes, and they immediately grew quite clear, and he could see as well as ever.

He took her to his kingdom, where he was received with joy. There they married and lived long and happily together.

CLEVER ELSA

THERE was once a Man who had a daughter called Clever Elsa. When she was grown up, her Father said: "We must get her married."

"Yes," said her Mother; "if only somebody came who would have her."

At last a suitor, named Hans, came from a distance. He made an offer for her on condition that she really was as clever as she was said to be.

"Oh!" said her Father, "she is a long-headed lass."

And her Mother said: "She can see the wind blowing in the street, and hear the flies coughing."

"Well," said Hans, "if she is not really clever, I won't have her."

When they were at dinner, her Mother said: "Elsa, go to the cellar and draw some beer."

Clever Elsa took the jug from the nail on the wall, and went to the cellar, clattering the lid as she went, to pass the time. When she reached the cellar she placed a chair near the cask so that she need not hurt her back by stooping. Then she put the jug before her and turned the tap.

And while the beer was running, so as not to be idle, she let her eyes rove all over the place, looking this way and that.

Suddenly she discovered a pickaxe just above her head, which a mason had by chance left hanging among the rafters.

Clever Elsa burst into tears, and said: "If I marry Hans, and we have a child, when it grows big, and we send it down to draw beer, the pickaxe will fall on its head and kill it." So there she sat crying and lamenting loudly at the impending mishap.

The others sat upstairs waiting for the beer, but Clever Elsa never came back.

Then the Mistress said to her Servant: "Go down to the cellar, and see why Elsa does not come back."

The Maid went, and found Elsa sitting by the cask, weeping bitterly. "Why, Elsa, whatever are you crying for?" she asked.

"Alas!" she answered, "have I not cause to cry? If I marry Hans, and we have a child, when he grows big, and we send him down to draw beer, perhaps that pickaxe will fall on his head and kill him."

Then the Maid said: "What a Clever Elsa we have"; and she, too, sat down by Elsa, and began to cry over the misfortune.

After a time, as the Maid did not come back, and they were growing very thirsty, the Master said to the Serving-man: "Go down to the cellar and see what has become

of Elsa and the Maid."

The Man went down, and there sat Elsa and the Maid weeping together. So he said: "What are you crying for?"

"Alas!" said Elsa, "have I not enough to cry for? If I marry Hans, and we have a child, and we send it when it is big enough into the cellar, to draw beer, the pickaxe will fall on its head and kill it."

The man said: "What a Clever Elsa we have"; and he, too, joined them and howled in company.

The people upstairs waited a long time for the Serving-man, but as he did not come back, the Husband said to his Wife: "Go down to the cellar yourself, and see what has become of Elsa."

So the Mistress went down and found all three making loud lamentations, and she asked the cause of their grief.

Then Elsa told her that her future child would be killed by the falling of the pickaxe when it was big enough to be sent to draw the beer. Her Mother said with the others: "Did you ever see such a Clever Elsa as we have?"

Her Husband upstairs waited some time, but as his Wife did not return, and his thirst grew greater, he said: "I must go to the cellar myself to see what has become of Elsa."

But when he got to the cellar, and found all the others sitting together in tears, caused by the fear that a child which Elsa might one day have, if she married Hans, might be killed by the falling of the pickaxe, when it went to draw beer, he too cried—

"What a Clever Elsa we have!"

Then he, too, sat down and added his lamentations to theirs.

The bridegroom waited alone upstairs for a long time; then, as nobody came back, he thought: "They must be waiting for me down there. I must go and see what they are doing."

So down he went, and when he found them all crying and lamenting in a heart-breaking manner, each one louder than the other, he asked: "What misfortune can possibly have happened?"

"Alas, dear Hans!" said Elsa, "if we marry and have a child, and we send it to draw beer when it is big enough, it may be killed if that pickaxe left hanging there were to fall on its head. Have we not cause to lament?"

"Well," said Hans, "more wits than this I do not need; and as you are such a Clever Elsa I will have you for my wife."

He took her by the hand, led her upstairs, and they celebrated the marriage.

When they had been married for a while, Hans said: "Wife, I will to work to earn some money; do you go into the fields and cut the corn, so that we may have some bread."

"Yes, my dear Hans; I will go at once."

When Hans had gone out, she made some good broth and took it into the field with her.

When she got there, she said to herself: "What shall I do, reap first, or eat first? I will eat first."

So she ate up the bowl of broth, which she found very satisfying, so she said again: "Which shall I do, sleep first, or reap first? I will sleep first." So she lay down among the corn and went to sleep.

Hans had been home a long time, and no Elsa came, so he said: "What a Clever Elsa I have. She is so industrious, she does not even come home to eat."

But as she still did not come, and it was getting dusk, Hans went out to see how much corn she had cut. He found that she had not cut any at all, and that she was lying there fast asleep. Hans hurried home to fetch a fowler's net with little bells on it, and this he hung around her without waking her. Then he ran home, shut the house door, and sat down to work.

At last, when it was quite dark, Clever Elsa woke up, and when she got up there was such a rattling, and the bells jingled at every step she took. She was terribly frightened, and wondered whether she really was Clever Elsa or not, and said: "Is it I, or is it not I?"

But she did not know what to answer, and stood for a time doubtful. At last she thought: "I will go home, and ask if it is I, or if it is not I; they will be sure to know."

She ran to the house, but found the door locked; so she knocked at the window, and cried: "Hans, is Elsa at home?"

"Yes," answered Hans, "she is!"

GRIMMS' FAIRY TALES

Then she started and cried: "Alas! then it is not I," and she went to another door; but when the people heard the jingling of the bells, they would not open the door, and nowhere would they take her in.

So she ran away out of the village, and was never seen again.

BRIAR ROSE
(The Sleeping Beauty)

A LONG time ago there lived a King and Queen, who said every day, "If only we had a child"; but for a long time they had none.

It fell out once, as the Queen was bathing, that a frog crept out of the water on to the land, and said to her: "Your wish shall be fulfilled; before a year has passed you shall bring a daughter into the world."

The frog's words came true. The Queen had a little girl who was so beautiful that the King could not contain himself for joy, and prepared a great feast. He invited not only his relations, friends, and acquaintances, but the fairies, in order that they might be favourably and kindly disposed towards the child. There were thirteen of them in the kingdom, but as the King had only twelve golden plates for them to eat off, one of the fairies had to stay at home.

The feast was held with all splendour, and when it came to an end the fairies all presented the child with a magic gift. One gave her virtue, another beauty, a third riches, and so on, with everything in the world that she could wish for.

When eleven of the fairies had said their say, the thirteenth suddenly appeared. She wanted to revenge herself for not having been invited. Without greeting anyone, or even glancing at the company, she called out in a loud voice: "The Princess shall prick herself with a distaff in her fifteenth year and shall fall down dead"; and without another word she turned and left the hall.

Everyone was terror-struck, but the twelfth fairy, whose wish was still unspoken, stepped forward. She could not cancel the curse, but could only soften it, so she said: "It shall not be death, but a deep sleep lasting a hundred years, into which your daughter shall fall."

The King was so anxious to guard his dear child from the misfortune, that he sent out a command that all the distaffs in the whole kingdom should be burned.

All the promises of the fairies came true.

The Princess grew up so beautiful, modest, kind, and clever that everyone who saw her could not but love her. Now it happened that on the very day when she was fifteen years old the King and Queen were away from home, and the Princess was left quite alone in the castle. She wandered about over the whole place, looking at rooms and halls as she pleased, and at last she came to an old tower. She ascended a narrow, winding staircase and reached a little door. A rusty key was sticking in the lock, and when she turned it the door flew open. In a little room sat an old woman with a spindle, spinning her flax busily.

"Good day, Granny," said the Princess; "what are you doing?"

"I am spinning," said the old woman, and nodded her head.

"What is the thing that whirls round so merrily?" asked the Princess; and she took the spindle and tried to spin too.

But she had scarcely touched it before the curse was fulfilled, and she pricked her finger with the spindle. The instant she felt the prick she fell upon the bed which was standing near, and lay still in a deep sleep which spread over the whole castle.

The King and Queen, who had just come home and had stepped into the hall, went to sleep, and all their courtiers with them. The horses went to sleep in the stable, the dogs in the yard, the doves on the roof, the flies on the wall; yes, even the fire flickering on the hearth grew still and went to sleep, and the roast meat stopped crackling; and the cook, who was pulling the scullion's hair because he had made some mistake, let him go and went to sleep. And the wind dropped, and on the trees in front of the castle not a leaf stirred.

But round the castle a hedge of briar roses began to grow up; every year it grew higher, till at last it surrounded the whole castle so that nothing could be seen of it, not even the flags on the roof.

But there was a legend in the land about the lovely sleeping Briar Rose, as the King's daughter was called, and from time to time princes came and tried to force a way through the hedge into the castle. But they found it impossible, for the thorns, as though they had hands, held them fast, and the princes remained caught in them without being able to free themselves, and so died a miserable death.

After many, many years a Prince came again to the country and heard an old man tell of the castle which stood behind the briar hedge, in which a most beautiful maiden called Briar Rose had been asleep for the last hundred years, and with her slept the King, Queen, and all her courtiers. He knew also, from his grandfather, that many princes had already come and sought to pierce through the briar hedge, and had remained caught in it and died a sad death.

Then the young Prince said, "I am not afraid; I am determined to go and look upon the lovely Briar Rose."

The good old man did all in his power to dissuade him, but the Prince would not listen to his words.

Now, however, the hundred years were just ended, and the day had come when Briar Rose was to wake up again. When the Prince approached the briar hedge it was in blossom, and was covered with beautiful large flowers which made way for him of their own accord and let him pass unharmed, and then closed up again into a hedge behind him.

In the courtyard he saw the horses and dappled hounds lying asleep, on the roof sat the doves with their heads under their wings: and when he went into the house the flies were asleep on the walls, and near the throne lay the King and Queen; in the kitchen was the cook, with his hand raised as though about to strike the scullion, and the maid sat with the black fowl before her which she was about to pluck.

He went on further, and all was so still that he could hear his own breathing. At last he reached the tower, and opened the door into the little room where Briar Rose was asleep. There she lay, looking so beautiful that he could not take his eyes off her; he bent down and gave her a kiss. As he touched her, Briar Rose opened her eyes and looked quite sweetly at him. Then they went down together; and the King woke up, and the Queen, and all the courtiers, and looked at each other with astonished eyes. The horses in the stable stood up and shook themselves, the hounds leaped about and wagged their tails, the doves on the roof lifted their heads from under their wings, looked round, and flew into the fields; the flies on the walls began to crawl again, the fire in the kitchen roused itself and blazed up and cooked the food, the meat began to crackle, and the cook boxed the scullion's ears so soundly that he screamed aloud, while the maid finished plucking the fowl. Then the wedding of the Prince and Briar Rose was celebrated with all splendour, and they lived happily till they died.

RUMPELSTILTSKIN

THERE was once a Miller who was very poor, but he had a beautiful daughter. Now, it fell out that he had occasion to speak with the King, and, in order to give himself an air of importance, he said: "I have a daughter who can spin gold out of straw."

The King said to the Miller: "That is an art in which I am much interested. If your daughter is as skillful as you say she is, bring her to my castle tomorrow, and I will put her to the test."

Accordingly, when the girl was brought to the castle, the King conducted her to a chamber which was quite full of straw, gave her a spinning-wheel and winder, and said, "Now, set to work, and if between tonight and tomorrow at dawn you have not spun this straw into gold you must die." Thereupon he carefully locked the door of the chamber, and she remained alone.

There sat the unfortunate Miller's daughter, and for the life of her did not know what to do. She had not the least idea how to spin straw into gold, and she became more and more distressed, until at last she began to weep. Then all at once the door sprang open, and in stepped a little Mannikin, who said: "Good evening, Mistress Miller, what are you weeping so for?"

"Alas!" answered the Maiden, "I've got to spin gold out of straw, and don't know how to do it."

Then the Mannikin said, "What will you give me if I spin it for you?"

"My necklace," said the Maid.

The little Man took the necklace, sat down before the spinning-wheel, and whir—whir—whir, in a trice the reel was full.

Then he fixed another reel, and whir—whir—whir, thrice round, and that too was full; and so it went on until morning, when all the straw was spun and all the reels were full of gold.

Immediately at sunrise the King came, and when he saw the gold he was astonished and much pleased, but his mind became only the more avaricious. So he had the Miller's daughter taken to another chamber, larger than the former one, and full of straw, and he ordered her to spin it also in one night, as she valued her life.

The Maiden was at her wits' end, and began to weep. Then again the door sprang open, and the little Mannikin appeared, and said, "What will you give me if I spin the straw into gold for you?"

"The ring off my finger," answered the Maiden.

The little Man took the ring, began to whir again at the wheel, and had by morning spun all the straw into gold.

The King was delighted at sight of the masses of gold, but was not even yet satisfied. So he had the Miller's daughter taken to a still larger chamber, full of straw, and said, "This must you tonight spin into gold, but if you succeed you shall become my Queen." "Even if she is only a Miller's daughter," thought he, "I shan't find a richer woman in the whole world."

When the girl was alone the little Man came again, and said for the third time, "What will you give me if I spin the straw for you this time?"

"I have nothing more that I can give," answered the girl.

"Well, promise me your first child if you become Queen."

"Who knows what may happen," thought the Miller's daughter; but she did not see any other way of getting out of the difficulty, so she promised the little Man what he demanded, and in return he spun the straw into gold once more.

When the King came in the morning, and found everything as he had wished, he celebrated his marriage with her, and the Miller's daughter became Queen.

About a year afterwards a beautiful child was born, but the Queen had forgotten all about the little Man. However, he suddenly entered her chamber, and said, "Now, give me what you promised."

The Queen was terrified, and offered the little Man all the wealth of the kingdom if he would let her keep the child. But the Mannikin said, "No, I would rather have some living thing than all the treasures of the world." Then the Queen began to moan and weep to such an extent that the little Man felt sorry for her. "I will give you three days," said he, "and if you discover my name within that time you shall keep the child."

Then during the night the Queen called to mind all the names that she had ever heard, and sent a messenger all over the country to inquire far and wide what other names there were. When the little Man came on the next day, she began with Caspar, Melchior, Balzer, and mentioned all the names which she knew, one after the other; but at every one the little Man said: "No; that's not my name."

The second day she had inquiries made all round the neighbourhood for the names of people living there,

and suggested to the little Man all the most unusual and strange names.

"Perhaps your name is Cowribs, Spindleshanks, or Lacelegs?"

But he answered every time, "No; that's not my name."

On the third day the messenger came back and said: "I haven't been able to find any new names, but as I came round the corner of a wood on a lofty mountain, where the Fox says good-night to the Hare, I saw a little house, and in front of the house a fire was burning; and around the fire an indescribably ridiculous little man was leaping, hopping on one leg, and singing:

> 'Today I bake; tomorrow I brew my beer;
> The next day I will bring the Queen's child here.
> Ah! lucky 'tis that not a soul doth know
> That Rumpelstiltskin is my name, ho! ho!'"

Then you can imagine how delighted the Queen was when she heard the name, and when presently afterwards the little Man came in and asked, "Now, your Majesty, what is my name?" at first she asked:

"Is your name Kunz?"

"No."

"Is it Heinz?"

"No."

"Is it, by chance, Rumpelstiltskin?"

"The devil told you that! The devil told you that!"

shrieked the little Man; and in his rage stamped his right foot into the ground so deep that he sank up to his waist.

Then, in his passion, he seized his left leg with both hands, and tore himself asunder in the middle.

THE ELVES AND THE SHOEMAKER

THERE was once a Shoemaker who, through no fault of his own, had become so poor that at last he had only leather enough left for one pair of shoes. At evening he cut out the shoes which he intended to begin upon the next morning, and since he had a good conscience, he lay down quietly, said his prayers, and fell asleep.

In the morning when he had said his prayers, and was preparing to sit down to work, he found the pair of shoes standing finished on his table. He was amazed, and could not understand it in the least.

He took the shoes in his hand to examine them more closely. They were so neatly sewn that not a stitch was out of place, and were as good as the work of a master-hand.

Soon after a purchaser came in, and as he was much pleased with the shoes, he paid more than the ordinary price for them, so that the Shoemaker was able to buy leather for two pairs of shoes with the money.

He cut them out in the evening, and next day, with fresh courage was about to go to work; but he had no need to, for when he got up, the shoes were finished, and buyers were not lacking. These gave him so much money that he was able to buy leather for four pairs of shoes.

Early next morning he found the four pairs finished, and so it went on; what he cut out at evening was finished in the morning, so that he was soon again in comfortable circumstances, and became a well-to-do man.

Now it happened one evening, not long before Christmas, when he had cut out shoes as usual, that he said to his Wife: "How would it be if we were to sit up tonight to see who it is that lends us such a helping hand?"

The Wife agreed, lighted a candle, and they hid themselves in the corner of the room behind the clothes which were hanging there.

At midnight came two little naked men who sat down at the Shoemaker's table, took up the cut-out work, and began with their tiny fingers to stitch, sew, and hammer so neatly and quickly, that the Shoemaker could not believe his eyes. They did not stop till everything was quite finished, and stood complete on the table; then they ran swiftly away.

The next day the Wife said: "The little men have made us rich, and we ought to show our gratitude. They ran about with nothing on, and must freeze with cold. Now I will make them little shirts, coats, waistcoats, and hose, and will even knit them a pair of stockings, and you shall make them each a pair of shoes."

The Husband agreed, and at evening, when they had everything ready, they laid out the presents on the table, and hid themselves to see how the little men would behave.

At midnight they came skipping in, and were about to set to work; but, instead of the leather already cut out, they found the charming little clothes.

At first they were surprised, then excessively delighted. With the greatest speed they put on and smoothed down the pretty clothes, singing:

> *"Now we're boys so fine and neat,*
> *Why cobble more for other's feet?"*

Then they hopped and danced about, and leapt over chairs and tables and out at the door. Henceforward, they came back no more, but the Shoemaker fared well as long as he lived, and had good luck in all his undertakings.

THE QUEEN BEE

ONCE upon a time two Princes started off in search of adventure, and falling into a wild, free mode of life, did not come home again.

The third brother, who was called Blockhead, set out to look for the other two. But when at last he found them, they mocked him for thinking of making his way in the world with his simplicity, while they, who were so much cleverer, could not get on.

They all three went on together till they came to an ant-heap. The two elder Princes wanted to disturb it, to see how the little ants crept away, carrying their eggs.

But Blockhead said: "Leave the little creatures alone. I will not allow you to disturb them."

Then they went on further till they came to a lake, in which a great many ducks were swimming about. The two wanted to catch and roast a pair.

But Blockhead would not allow it, and said: "Leave the creatures alone. You shall not kill them."

At last they came to a bee's nest, containing such a quantity of honey that it flowed round the trunk of the tree.

The two Princes wanted to set fire to the tree, and suffocate the bees, so as to remove the honey.

But Blockhead stopped them again, and said: "Leave the creatures alone. I will not let you burn them."

At last the three brothers came to a castle, where the stables were full of stone horses, but not a soul was to be seen. They went through all the rooms till they came to a door quite at the end, fastened with three bolts. In the middle of the door was a lattice, through which one could see into the room.

There they saw a little grey man sitting at a table. They called to him once—twice, but he did not hear them. Finally, when they had called him the third time, he stood up and opened the door, and came out. He said not a word, but led them to a richly-spread table, and when they had eaten and drunk, he took them each to a bedroom.

The next morning the little grey man came to the eldest Prince, beckoned, and led him to a stone tablet whereon were inscribed three tasks by means of which the castle should be freed from enchantment.

This was the first task: In the wood, under the moss, lay the Princess's pearls, a thousand in number. These had all to be found, and if at sunset a single one were missing, the seeker was turned to stone.

The eldest went away, and searched all day, but when evening came, he had only found the first hundred, and it happened as the inscription foretold. He was turned to stone.

The next day the second brother undertook the quest. But he fared no better than the first, for he only found two hundred pearls, and he too was turned to stone.

At last came Blockhead's turn. He searched in the moss, but the pearls were hard to find, and he got on but slowly.

Then he sat down on a rock and cried, and as he was sitting there, the Ant-King, whose life he had saved, came up with five thousand ants, and it was not long before the little creatures had found all the pearls and laid them in a heap.

Now the second task was to get the key of the Princess's room out of the lake.

When Blockhead came to the lake, the ducks, which he had once saved, swam up, dived, and brought up the key from the depths.

But the third task was the hardest. The Prince had to find out which was the youngest and prettiest of the Princesses while they were asleep.

They were exactly alike, and could not be distinguished in any way, except that before going to sleep each had eaten a different kind of sweet. The eldest a piece of sugar, the second a little syrup, and the third a spoonful of honey.

Then the Queen of the Bees, whom Blockhead had saved from burning, came and tried the lips of all three. Finally, she settled on the mouth of the one who had eaten the honey, and so the Prince recognized the right one.

Then the charm was broken and everything in the castle was set free, and those who had been turned to stone took human form again.

And Blockhead married the youngest and sweetest Princess, and became King after her father's death, while his two brothers married the other sisters.

KING THRUSHBEARD

THERE was once a King who had a Daughter. She was
more beautiful than words can tell, but at the same time
so proud and haughty that no man who came to woo
her was good enough for her. She turned away one after
another, and even mocked them.

One day her father ordered a great feast to be given,
and invited all the marriageable young men from far and
near.

They were all placed in a row, according to their rank
and position. First came Kings, then Dukes, then Princes,
Earls, and Barons.

The Princess was led through the ranks, but she had
some fault to find with all of them.

One was too stout. "That barrel!" she said. The next
was too tall. "Long and lean is no good!" The third was
too short. "Short and stout, can't turn about!" The fourth
was too white. "Pale as death!" The fifth was too red.
"Turkey-cock!" The sixth was not straight. "Oven-dried!"

So there was something against each of them. But
she made specially merry over one good King, who stood
quite at the head of the row, and whose chin was a little
crooked.

"Why!" she cried, "he has a chin like the beak of a thrush."

After that, he was always called "King Thrushbeard."

When the old King saw that his Daughter only made fun of them, and despised all the suitors who were assembled, he was very angry, and swore that the first beggar who came to the door should be her husband.

A few days after, a wandering Musician began to sing at the window, hoping to receive charity.

When the King heard him, he said: "Let him be brought in."

The Musician came in, dressed in dirty rags, and sang to the King and his Daughter, and when he had finished, he begged alms of them.

The King said: "Your song has pleased me so much, that I will give you my Daughter to be your wife."

The Princess was horror-stricken. But the King said: "I have sworn an oath to give you to the first beggar who came; and I will keep my word."

No entreaties were of any avail. A Parson was brought, and she had to marry the Musician there and then.

When the marriage was completed, the King said: "Now you are a beggar-woman, you can't stay in my castle any longer. You must go away with your Husband."

The Beggar took her by the hand and led her away, and she was obliged to go with him on foot.

When they came to a big wood, she asked:

"Ah, who is the Lord of this forest so fine?"
"It belongs to King Thrushbeard. It might have been thine,
  If his Queen you had been."
"Ah! poor young thing!
  I would I'd accepted the hand of the King."

After that they reached a great meadow, and she asked again:

"Ah! who is the Lord of these meadows so fine?"
"They belong to King Thrushbeard, and would have been thine,
  If his Queen you had been."
"Ah! poor young thing!
  I would I'd accepted the love of the King."

Then they passed through a large town,. and again she asked:

"Ah! who is the Lord of this city so fine?"
"It belongs to King Thrushbeard, and it might have been thine,
  If his Queen you had been."
"Ah! poor young thing!
  I would I'd accepted the heart of the King."

"It doesn't please me at all," said the Musician, "that you are always wishing for another husband. Am I not good enough for you?"

At last they came to a miserable little hovel, and she said:

"Ah, heavens! what's this house, so low and small?
  This wretched, puny hut's no house at all."

The Musician answered: "This is my house, and yours; where we are to live together."

The door was so low that she had to stoop down to get in.

"Where are the servants?" asked the Princess.

"Servants indeed!" answered the Beggar. "Whatever you want done, you must do for yourself. Light the fire, and put on the kettle to make my supper. I am very tired."

But the Princess knew nothing about lighting fires or cooking, and to get it done at all, the Beggar had to do it himself.

When they had finished their humble fare, they went to bed. But in the morning the Man made her get up very early to do the housework.

They lived like this for a few days, till they had eaten up all their store of food.

Then the Man said: "Wife, this won't do any longer. We can't live here without working. You shall make baskets."

So he went out and cut some willow twigs, and brought them home. She began to weave them, but they bruised her tender hands.

"I see that won't do," said the Beggar. "You had better spin. Perhaps you can manage that."

So she sat down and tried to spin, but the harsh yarn soon cut her delicate fingers and made them bleed.

"Now you see," said the Man, "what a good-for-nothing you are. I have made a bad bargain in you. But I will try to start a trade in earthenware. You must sit in the market and offer your goods for sale."

"Alas!" she thought, "if any of the people from my father's kingdom come and see me sitting in the market-place, offering goods for sale, they will scoff at me." But it was no good. She had to obey, unless she meant to die of hunger.

All went well the first time. The people willingly bought her wares because she was so handsome, and they paid what she asked them—nay, some even gave her the money and left her the pots as well.

They lived on the gains as long as they lasted, and then the Man laid in a new stock of wares.

She took her seat in a corner of the market, set out her crockery about her, and began to cry her wares.

Suddenly, a Hussar came galloping up, and rode right in among the pots, breaking them into thousands of bits.

She began to cry, and was so frightened that she did not know what to do. "Oh! what will become of me?" she cried. "What will my Husband say to me?" She ran home, and told him her misfortune.

"Who would ever think of sitting at the corner of the market with crockery?" he said. "Stop that crying. I see you are no manner of use for any decent kind of work. I have been to our King's palace, and asked if they do not want a kitchen wench, and they have promised to try you. You will get your victuals free, at any rate."

So the Princess became a kitchen wench, and had to wait upon the Cook and do all the dirty work. She fixed a pot into each of her pockets, and in them took home her share of the scraps and leavings, and upon these they lived.

It so happened that the marriage of the eldest Princess just then took place, and the poor Woman went upstairs and stood behind the door to peep at all the splendour.

When the rooms were lighted up, and she saw the guests streaming in, one more beautiful than the other, and the scene grew more and more brilliant, she thought, with a heavy heart, of her sad fate. She cursed the pride and haughtiness which had been the cause of her humiliation, and of her being brought to such depths.

Every now and then the Servants would throw her bits from the savoury dishes they were carrying away from the feast, and these she put into her pots to take home with her.

All at once the King came in. He was dressed in silk and velvet, and he had a golden chain round his neck.

When he saw the beautiful Woman standing at the door, he seized her by the hand, and wanted to dance with her.

But she shrank and refused, because she saw that it was King Thrushbeard, who had been one of the suitors for her hand, and whom she had most scornfully driven away.

Her resistance was no use, and he dragged her into

the hall. The string by which her pockets were suspended broke. Down fell the pots, and the soup and savoury morsels were spilt all over the floor.

When the guests saw it, they burst into shouts of mocking laughter.

She was so ashamed, that she would gladly have sunk into the earth. She rushed to the door, and tried to escape, but on the stairs a Man stopped her and brought her back.

When she looked at him, it was no other than King Thrushbeard again.

He spoke kindly to her, and said: "Do not be afraid. I and the Beggar-Man, who lived in the poor little hovel with you, are one and the same. For love of you I disguised myself; and I was also the Hussar who rode among your pots. All this I did to bend your proud spirit, and to punish you for the haughtiness with which you mocked me."

She wept bitterly, and said: "I was very wicked, and I am not worthy to be your wife."

But he said: "Be happy! Those evil days are over. Now we will celebrate our true wedding."

The waiting-women came and put rich clothing upon her, and her Father, with all his Court, came and wished her joy on her marriage with King Thrushbeard.

Then her true happiness began. I wish we had been there to see it, you and I.

RED RIDING HOOD

THERE was once a sweet little maiden, who was loved by all who knew her. But she was especially dear to her Grandmother, who did not know how to make enough of the child. Once she gave her a little red velvet cloak. It was so becoming, and the little girl liked it so much, that she would never wear anything else; and so she got the name of Red Riding Hood.

One day her Mother said to her: "Come here, Red Riding Hood, take this cake and a bottle of wine to Grandmother. She is weak and ill, and they will do her good. Go quickly, before it gets hot, and don't loiter by the way, or run, or you will fall down and break the bottle, and there would be no wine for Grandmother. When you get there, don't forget to say 'Good morning' prettily, without staring about you."

"I will do just as you tell me," Red Riding Hood promised her Mother.

Her Grandmother lived away in the woods, a good half-hour from the village. When she got to the wood, she met a Wolf. But Red Riding Hood did not know what a wicked animal he was, so she was not a bit afraid of him.

"Good morning, Red Riding Hood," he said.

"Good morning, Wolf," she answered.

"Where are you going so early, Red Riding Hood?"

"To Grandmother's."

"What have you got in your basket?"

"Cake and wine; we baked yesterday, so I'm taking a cake to Grannie. She wants something to make her well."

"Where does your Grandmother live, Red Riding Hood?"

"A good quarter of an hour further into the wood. Her house stands under three big oak trees, near a hedge of nut trees which you must know," said Red Riding Hood.

The Wolf thought: "This tender little creature will be a plump morsel; she will be nicer than the old woman. I must be cunning, and snap them both up."

He walked along with Red Riding Hood for a while, then he said: "Look at the pretty flowers, Red Riding Hood. Why don't you look about you? I don't believe you even hear the birds sing. You are just as solemn as if you were going to school. Everything else is so gay out here in the woods."

Red Riding Hood raised her eyes, and when she saw the sunlight dancing through the trees, and all the bright flowers, she thought: "I'm sure Grannie would be pleased if I took her a bunch of fresh flowers. It is still quite early, I shall have plenty of time to pick them."

So she left the path, and wandered off among the trees to pick the flowers. Each time she picked one, she always saw another prettier one further on. So she went deeper

137

and deeper into the forest.

In the meantime the Wolf went straight off to the Grandmother's cottage, and knocked at the door.

"Who is there?"

"Red Riding Hood, bringing you a cake and some wine. Open the door!"

"Press the latch!" cried the old woman. "I am too weak to get up."

The Wolf pressed the latch, and the door sprang open. He went straight in and up to the bed without saying a word, and ate up the poor old woman. Then he put on her nightdress and nightcap, got into bed and drew the curtains.

Red Riding Hood ran about picking flowers till she could carry no more, and then she remembered her Grandmother again. She was astonished when she got to the house to find the door open, and when she entered the room everything seemed so strange.

She felt quite frightened, but she did not know why. "Generally I like coming to see Grandmother so much," she thought. She cried: "Good morning, Grandmother," but she received no answer.

Then she went up to the bed and drew the curtain back. There lay her Grandmother, but she had drawn her cap down over her face, and she looked very odd.

"Oh, Grandmother, what big ears you have got," she said.

"The better to hear with, my dear."

"Grandmother, what big eyes you have got."

"The better to see with, my dear."

"What big hands you have got, Grandmother."

"The better to catch hold of you with, my dear."

"But, Grandmother, what big teeth you have got."

"The better to eat you up with, my dear."

Hardly had the Wolf said this, than he made a spring out of bed, and devoured poor little Red Riding Hood. When the Wolf had satisfied himself, he went back to bed and he was soon snoring loudly.

A Huntsman went past the house, and thought, "How loudly the old lady is snoring; I must see if there is anything the matter with her."

So he went into the house, and up to the bed, where he found the Wolf fast asleep. "Do I find you here, you old sinner?" he said. "Long enough have I sought you."

He raised his gun to shoot, when it just occurred to him that perhaps the Wolf had eaten up the old lady, and that she might still be saved. So he took a knife and began cutting open the sleeping Wolf. At first he saw the red cloak, and then, the little girl sprang out, and cried: "Oh, how frightened I was, it was so dark inside the Wolf!" Next the old Grandmother came out, alive, but hardly able to breathe.

Red Riding Hood brought some big stones with which they filled the Wolf, so that when he woke and tried to spring away, they dragged him back, and he fell down dead.

They were all quite happy now. The Huntsman skinned the Wolf, and took the skin home. The Grandmother ate the cake and drank the wine which Red Riding Hood had brought, and she soon felt quite strong. Red Riding Hood thought; "I will never again wander off into the forest as long as I live, if my Mother forbids it."

THE GOLDEN GOOSE

THERE was once a man who had three sons. The youngest of them was called Simpleton. He was scorned and despised by the others, and kept in the background.

The eldest son was going into the forest to cut wood, and, before he started, his mother gave him a nice sweet cake and a bottle of wine to take with him, so that he might not suffer from hunger or thirst. In the wood he met a little, old, grey man, who bade him good-day, and said, "Give me a bit of the cake in your pocket, and let me have a drop of your wine. I am so hungry and thirsty."

But the clever son said, "If I give you my cake and wine, I shan't have enough for myself. Be off with you."

He left the little Man standing there, and went on his way. But he had not been long at work, cutting down a tree, before he made a false stroke, and dug the axe into his own arm, and he was obliged to go home to have it bound up.

Now, this was no accident; it was brought about by the little grey Man.

The second son now had to go into the forest to cut wood, and, like the eldest, his mother gave him a sweet cake and a bottle of wine. In the same way the little grey Man met him, and asked for a piece of his cake and a drop of his wine. But the second son made the same

sensible answer, "If I give you any, I shall have the less for myself. Be off out of my way," and he went on.

His punishment, however, was not long delayed. After a few blows at the tree, he hit his own leg, and had to be carried home.

Then Simpleton said, "Let me go to cut the wood, father."

But his father said, "Your brothers have only come to harm by it. You had better leave it alone. You know nothing about it." But Simpleton begged so hard to be allowed to go that at last his father said, "Well, off you go then. You will be wiser when you have hurt yourself."

His mother gave him a cake which was only mixed with water and baked in the ashes, and a bottle of sour beer. When he reached the forest, like the others, he met the little grey Man, who greeted him, and said, "Give me a bit of your cake and a drop of your wine. I am so hungry and thirsty."

Simpleton answered, "I only have a cake baked in the ashes, and some sour beer; but, if you like such fare, we will sit down and eat it together."

So they sat down; but when Simpleton pulled out his cake, it was a sweet, nice cake, and his sour beer was turned into good wine. So they ate and drank, and the little Man said, "As you have such a good heart, and are willing to share your goods, I will give you good luck. There stands an old tree: cut it down, and you will find something at the roots."

So saying he disappeared.

Simpleton cut down the tree, and when it fell, lo, and behold! a Goose was sitting among the roots, and its feathers were of pure gold. He picked it up, and taking it with him, went to an inn, where he meant to stay the night. The landlord had three daughters, who saw the Goose, and were very curious as to what kind of bird it could be, and wanted to get one of its golden feathers.

The eldest thought, "There will soon be some opportunity for me to pull out one of the feathers," and when Simpleton went outside, she took hold of its wing to pluck out a feather. But her hand stuck fast, and she could not get away.

Soon after, the second sister came up, meaning also to pluck out one of the golden feathers. But she had hardly touched her sister when she found herself held fast.

Lastly, the third one came, with the same intention, but the others screamed out, "Keep away! For goodness sake, keep away!"

But she, not knowing why she was to keep away, thought, "Why should I not be there, if they are there?"

So she ran up, but as soon as she touched her sisters she had to stay hanging on to them, and they all had to pass the night like this.

In the morning, Simpleton took up the Goose under his arm, without noticing the three girls hanging on behind. They had to keep running behind, dodging his legs right and left.

In the middle of the fields they met the Parson, who, when he saw the procession, cried out: "For shame, you bold girls! Why do you run after the lad like that? Do you call that proper behaviour?"

Then he took hold of the hand of the youngest girl to pull her away; but no sooner had he touched her than he felt himself held fast, and he, too, had to run behind.

Soon after the Sexton came up, and, seeing his master the Parson treading on the heels of the three girls, cried out in amazement, "Hallo, your Reverence! Whither away so fast? Don't forget that we have a christening!"

So saying, he plucked the Parson by the sleeve, and soon found that he could not get away.

As this party of five, one behind the other, tramped on, two Peasants came along the road, carrying their hoes. The Parson called them, and asked them to set the Sexton and himself free. But as soon as ever they touched the Sexton they were held fast, so now there were seven people running behind Simpleton and his Goose.

145

By-and-by they reached a town, where a King ruled whose only daughter was so solemn that nothing and nobody could make her laugh. So the King had proclaimed that whoever could make her laugh should marry her.

When Simpleton heard this he took his Goose, with all his following, before her, and when she saw these seven people running, one behind another, she burst into fits of laughter. It seemed as if she could never stop.

Thereupon Simpleton asked her in marriage. But the King did not like him for a son-in-law, and he made all sorts of conditions. First, he said Simpleton must bring him a man who could drink up a cellar full of wine.

Then Simpleton at once thought of the little grey Man who might be able to help him, and he went out to the forest to look for him. On the very spot where the tree that he had cut down had stood, he saw a Man sitting with a very sad face. Simpleton asked him what was the matter, and he answered:

"I am so thirsty, and I can't quench my thirst. I hate cold water, and I have already emptied a cask of wine. But what is a drop like that on a burning stone?"

"Well, there I can help you," said Simpleton. "Come with me, and you shall soon have enough to drink and to spare."

He led him to the King's cellar, and the Man drank and drank till his sides ached, and by the end of the day the casks were empty.

146

Then again Simpleton demanded his bride. But the King was annoyed that a wretched fellow called "Simpleton" should have his daughter, and he made new conditions. He was now to find a man who could eat up a mountain of bread.

Simpleton did not reflect long, but went straight to the forest, and there in the self-same place sat a Man tightening a strap round his body, and making a very miserable face. He said: "I have eaten up a whole ovenful of rolls, but what is the good of that when anyone is as hungry as I am. I am never satisfied. I have to tighten my belt every day if I am not to die of hunger."

Simpleton was delighted, and said: "Get up and come with me. You shall have enough to eat."

And he took him to the Court, where the King had caused all the flour in the kingdom to be brought together, and a huge mountain of bread to be baked. The Man from the forest sat down before it and began to eat, and at the end of the day the whole mountain had disappeared.

Now, for the third time, Simpleton asked for his bride. But again the King tried to find an excuse, and demanded a ship which could sail on land as well as at sea.

"As soon as you sail up in it, you shall have my daughter," he said.

Simpleton went straight to the forest, and there sat the little grey Man to whom he had given his cake. The little Man said: "I have eaten and drunk for you, and now I will give you the ship, too. I do it all because you were merciful to me."

Then he gave him the ship which could sail on land as well as at sea, and when the King saw it, he could no longer withhold his daughter. The marriage was celebrated, and, at the King's death, the Simpleton inherited the kingdom, and lived long and happily with his wife.

THE FOX AND THE HORSE

A PEASANT once had a faithful Horse, but it had grown old and could no longer do its work. Its master grudged it food, and said: "I can't use you anymore, but I still feel kindly towards you. If you show yourself strong enough to bring me a Lion, I will keep you to the end of your days. But away with you now, out of my stable." And he chased it out into the open country.

The poor Horse was very sad, and went into the forest to get a little shelter from the wind and weather. There he met a Fox, who said: "Why do you hang your head, and wander about in this solitary fashion?"

"Alas!" answered the Horse, "avarice and honesty cannot live together. My master has forgotten all the service I have done him for these many years, and because I can no longer plough he will no longer feed me, and he has chased me away."

"Without any consolation?" asked the Fox.

"A very poor consolation. He said if I was strong enough to bring him a Lion he would keep me. But he knows well enough that the task is beyond me."

The Fox said: "I will help you. Just lie down here, and stretch your legs out as if you were dead." The Horse did as he was told, and the Fox went to the Lion's den, not far off, and said: "There is a dead Horse out there. Come along with me, and you will have a rare meal." The Lion went with him, and when they got up to the Horse, the Fox said: "You can't eat it in comfort here. I'll tell you what. I will tie it to you, and you can drag it away to your den, and enjoy it at your leisure."

The plan pleased the Lion, and he stood quite still, close to the Horse, so that the Fox should fasten them together. But the Fox tied the Lion's legs together with the Horse's tail, and twisted and knotted it so that it would be quite impossible for it to come undone.

When he had finished his work he patted the Horse on the shoulder, and said: "Pull, old Grey! Pull!"

Then the Horse sprang up, and drew the Lion away behind him. The Lion in his rage roared, so that all the birds in the forest were terrified, and flew away. But the Horse let him roar, and never stopped till he stood before his master's door.

When the master saw him he was delighted, and said: "You shall stay with me, and have a good time as long as you live."

And he fed him well till he died.

THE THREE BROTHERS

THERE was once a man who had three sons, but no fortune except the house he lived in. Now, each of them wanted to have the house after his death; but their father was just as fond of one as of the other, and did not know how to treat them all fairly. He did not want to sell the house because it had belonged to his forefathers, or he might have divided the money between them.

At last an idea came into his head, and he said to his sons, "Go out into the world, and each learn a trade, and when you come home the one who makes best use of his handicraft shall have the house."

The sons were quite content with this plan, and the eldest decided to be a Blacksmith, the second a Barber, and the third a Fencing-Master. They fixed a time when they would all meet at home again, and then they set off.

It so happened that they each found a clever master with whom they learnt their business thoroughly. The Blacksmith shod the King's horses, and he thought, "I shall certainly be the one to have the house."

The Barber shaved nobody but grand gentlemen, so

he thought it would fall to him.

The Fencing-Master got many blows, but he set his teeth, and would not let himself be put out, because he thought, "If I am afraid of a blow, I shall never get the house."

Now, when the given time had passed, they all went home together to their Father. But they did not know how to get a good opportunity of showing off their powers, and sat down to discuss the matter.

Suddenly a hare came running over the field.

"Ah," cried the Barber, "she comes just in the nick of time."

He took up his bowl and his soap, and got his lather by the time the hare came quite close. Then he soaped her and shaved her as she raced along, without giving her a cut or missing a single hair. His Father said, "If the others don't look out, the house will be yours."

Before long, a gentleman came along in his carriage at full gallop.

"Now, Father, you shall see what I can do," said the Blacksmith. He ran after the carriage and tore the four shoes off the horse as he galloped along, and, without stopping a second, shod him with new ones.

"You are a fine fellow, indeed," said his Father. "You know your business as well as your brother. I don't know which I shall give the house to at this rate."

Then the third one said, "Let me have a chance too, Father."

As it was beginning to rain, he drew his sword and swirled it round and round his head, so that not a drop fell on him. Even when the rain grew heavier, so heavy that it seemed as if it was being poured from the sky out of buckets, he swung the sword faster and faster, and remained as dry as if he had been under a roof.

His Father was amazed, and said, "You have done the best. The house is yours."

Both the other brothers were quite satisfied with this decision. And as they were all so devoted to each other, they lived happily together in the same house for the rest of their lives.

THE SEVEN RAVENS

THERE was once a Man who had seven sons, but never a daughter, however much he wished for one.

At last, however, he had a daughter.

His joy was great, but the child was small and delicate, and, on account of her weakness, she was to be christened at home.

The Father sent one of his sons in haste to the spring to fetch some water; the other six ran with him, and because each of them wanted to be the first to draw the water, between them the pitcher fell into the brook.

There they stood and didn't know what to do, and not one of them ventured to go home.

As they did not come back, their Father became impatient, and said: "Perhaps the young rascals are playing about, and have forgotten it altogether."

He became anxious lest his little girl should die unbaptised, and in hot vexation, he cried: "I wish the youngsters would all turn into Ravens!"

Scarcely were the words uttered, when he heard a whirring in the air above his head, and, looking upwards, he saw seven coal-black Ravens flying away.

The parents could not recall the imprecation, and were very sad about the loss of their seven sons, but they consoled themselves in some measure with their dear little daughter, who soon became strong, and every day more beautiful.

For a long time she was unaware that she had had any brothers, for her parents took care not to mention it.

However, one day by chance she heard some people saying about her: "Oh yes, the girl's pretty enough; but you know she is really to blame for the misfortune of her seven brothers."

Then she became very sad, and went to her father and mother and asked if she had ever had any brothers, and what had become of them?

The parents could no longer conceal the secret. They said, however, that what had happened was by the decree of heaven, and that her birth was merely the innocent occasion.

But the little girl could not get the matter off her conscience for a single day, and thought that she was bound to release her brothers again. She had no peace or quiet until she had secretly set out, and gone forth into the wide world to trace her brothers, wherever they might be, and to free them, let it cost what it might.

She took nothing with her but a little ring as a remembrance of her parents, a loaf of bread against hunger, a pitcher of water against thirst, and a little chair in case of fatigue. She kept going on and on until she came to the end of the world.

Then she came to the Sun but it was hot and terrible. She ran hastily away to the Moon, but it was too cold, and, moreover, dismal and dreary.

Then she quickly made off, and came to the Stars, and they were kind and good, and everyone sat on his own special seat.

But the Morning Star stood up, and gave her a little bone, and said: "Unless you have this bone, you cannot open the glass mountain, and in the glass mountain are your brothers."

The girl took the bone, and wrapped it up carefully in a little kerchief, and went on again until she came to the glass mountain.

The gate was closed, and she meant to take out the little bone. But when she undid the kerchief it was empty, and she had lost the good Star's present.

How, now, was she to set to work? She was determined to rescue her brothers, but had no key to open the glass mountain.

The good little sister pushed her own tiny finger into the door, and succeeded in opening it.

When she had entered, she met a Dwarf, who said: "My child, what are you looking for?"

"I am looking for my brothers, the Seven Ravens," she answered.

The Dwarf said: "My masters, the Ravens, are not at home; but if you like to wait until they come, please walk in."

Thereupon the Dwarf brought in the Ravens' supper, on seven little plates, and in seven little cups, and the little sister ate a crumb or two from each of the little plates, and took a sip from each of the little cups, but she let the ring she had brought with her fall into the last little cup.

All at once a whirr and a cry was heard in the air; then the Dwarf said: "Now my masters the Ravens are coming flying home."

Then they came in, and wanted to eat and drink, and began to look about for their little plates and cups.

But they said one after another: "Halloa! who has been eating off my plate? Who has been drinking out of my cup? There has been some human mouth here."

And when the seventh came to the bottom of his cup, the ring rolled up against his lips.

Then he looked at it, and recognised it as a ring belonging to his father and mother, and said: "God grant that our sister may be here, and that we may be delivered."

As the maiden was standing behind the door listening, she heard the wish and came forward. Then all the Ravens got back their human form again.

And they embraced and kissed one another, and went joyfully home.

THE GOLDEN BIRD

A LONG time ago there was a King who had a lovely pleasure-garden round his palace, and in it stood a tree which bore golden apples. When the apples were nearly ripe they were counted, but the very next morning one was missing.

This was reported to the King, and he ordered a watch to be set every night under the tree.

The King had three sons, and he sent the eldest into the garden at nightfall. But by midnight he was overcome with sleep, and in the morning another apple was missing.

On the following night the second son had to keep watch, but he fared no better. When the clock struck twelve, he too was fast asleep, and in the morning another apple was gone.

The turn to watch now came to the third son. He was quite ready, but the King had not much confidence in him, and thought that he would accomplish even less than his brothers. At last, however, he gave his permission. So the youth lay down under the tree to watch, determined not to let sleep get the mastery over him.

As the clock struck twelve there was a rustling in the air, and by the light of the moon he saw a Bird, whose shining feathers were of pure gold. The Bird settled on the tree, and was just plucking an apple when the young Prince shot an arrow at it. The Bird flew away, but the arrow hit its plumage, and one of the golden feathers fell to the ground. The Prince picked it up, and in the morning took it to the King and told him all that he had seen in the night.

The King assembled his council, and everybody declared that a feather like that was worth more than the whole kingdom. "If the feather is worth so much," said the King, "one will not satisfy me; I must and will have the whole Bird."

The eldest, relying on his cleverness, set out in search of the Bird, and thought that he would be sure to find it soon.

When he had gone some distance he saw a Fox sitting on the outskirts of a wood; he raised his gun and aimed at it. The Fox cried out, "Do not shoot me, and I will give you some good advice. You are going to look for the Golden Bird. You will come to a village at nightfall, where you will find two inns opposite each other. One of them will be brightly lighted, and there will be noise and revelry going on in it. Be sure you do not choose that one, but go into the other, even if you don't like the look of it as well."

"How can a stupid animal like that give me good advice?" thought the King's son, and he pulled the trigger, but missed the Fox, who turned tail and made off into the wood.

Thereupon the Prince continued his journey, and at nightfall reached the village with the two inns. Singing and dancing were going on in the one, and the other had a poverty-stricken and decayed appearance.

"I should be a fool," he said, "if I were to go to that miserable place with this good one so near."

So he went into the noisy one, and lived there in rioting and revelry, forgetting the Bird, his father, and all his good counsels.

When some time had passed and the eldest son did not come back, the second prepared to start in quest of the Golden Bird. He met the Fox, as the eldest son had done, and it gave him the same good advice, of which he took just as little heed.

He came to the two inns, and saw his brother standing at the window of the one whence sounds of revelry proceeded. He could not withstand his brother's calling, so he went in and gave himself up to a life of pleasure.

Again some time passed, and the King's youngest son wanted to go out to try his luck; but his father would not let him go.

"It is useless," he said. "He will be even less able to find the Golden Bird than his brothers, and when any ill luck overtakes him, he will not be able to help himself. He has no backbone."

But at last, because the boy gave him no peace, the King let him go. The Fox again sat at the edge of the wood, begged for its life, and gave its good advice. The Prince was good-natured, and said: "Be calm, little Fox, I will do thee no harm."

"You won't repent it," answered the Fox; "and so that you may get along faster, come and mount on my tail."

No sooner had he seated himself than the Fox began to run, and away they flew over stock and stone, at such a pace that his hair whistled in the wind.

When they reached the village, the Prince dismounted, and followed the good advice of the Fox. He went straight to the mean inn without looking about him, and there he passed a peaceful night. In the morning when he went out into the fields, there sat the Fox, who said: "I will now tell you what you must do next. Walk straight on till you come to a castle, in front of which a whole regiment of soldiers is encamped. Don't be afraid of them; they will all be asleep and snoring. Walk through the midst of them straight into the castle, and through all the rooms, and at last you will reach an apartment where the Golden Bird will be hanging in a common wooden cage. A golden cage stands near it for show, but beware! Whatever you do, you must not take the bird out of the wooden cage to put it into the other, or it will be the worse for you."

After these words the Fox again stretched out his tail, the Prince took his seat on it, and away they flew over

stock and stone, till his hair whistled in the wind.

When he arrived at the castle, he found everything just as the Fox had said.

The Prince went to the room where the Golden Bird hung in the wooden cage, with a golden cage standing by, and the three golden apples were scattered about the room. He thought it would be absurd to leave the beautiful Bird in the common old cage, so he opened the door, caught it, and put it into the golden cage. But as he did it, the Bird uttered a piercing-shriek. The soldiers woke up, rushed in, and carried him away to prison. Next morning he was taken before a judge, and, as he confessed all, he was sentenced to death. The King, however, said that he would spare his life on one condition, and this was that he should bring him the Golden Horse which runs faster than the wind. In addition, he should have the Golden Bird as a reward.

So the Prince set off with many sighs. He was very sad, for where was he to find the Golden Horse?

Then suddenly he saw his old friend the Fox sitting on the road. "Now you see," said the Fox, "all this has happened because you did not listen to me. All the same, keep up your spirits. I will protect you and tell you how to find the Golden Horse. You must keep straight along the road, and you will come to a palace, in the stable of which stands the Golden Horse. The grooms will be lying round the stable, but they will be fast asleep and snoring, and you can safely lead the horse through them. But one thing you must beware of. Put the old saddle of wood and leather upon it, and not the golden one hanging near, or you will rue it."

Then the Fox stretched out his tail, the Prince took his seat, and away they flew over stock and stone, till his hair whistled in the wind.

Everything happened just as the Fox had said. The Prince came to the stable where the Golden Horse stood, but when he was about to put the old saddle on its back, he thought, "Such a beautiful animal will be disgraced if I don't put the good saddle upon him, which he deserves." But hardly had the golden saddle touched the horse than he began neighing loudly. The grooms awoke, seized the Prince, and threw him into a dungeon.

The next morning he was taken before a judge, and condemned to death. But the King promised to spare his life, and give him the Golden Horse as well, if he could bring him the beautiful Princess out of the golden palace. With a heavy heart the Prince set out, but to his delight he soon met the faithful Fox.

"I ought to leave you to your fate," he said; "but I will have pity on you and once more help you out of your trouble. Your road leads straight to the golden palace. You will reach it in the evening; and at night, when everything is quiet, the beautiful Princess will go to take a bath. As she walks through the halls, spring forward and give her a kiss, and she will follow you. Lead her away with you. But on no account allow her to bid her parents good-bye, or it will go badly with you."

Again the Fox stretched out his tail. The Prince seated himself upon it, and off they flew over stock and stone, till his hair whistled in the wind.

When he got to the palace, it was just as the Fox had said. He waited till midnight, and when the whole palace was wrapped in sleep, and the maiden went to take a bath, he sprang forward and gave her a kiss. She said she was quite willing to go with him, but she implored him to let her say good-bye to her parents. At first he refused; but as she cried, and fell at his feet, at last he gave her leave. Hardly had the maiden stepped up to her father's bed, when he and everyone else in the palace woke up. The Prince was seized, and thrown into prison.

Next morning the King said to him, "Your life is forfeited, and it can only be spared if you clear away the mountain in front of my window, which shuts out the view. It must be done in eight days, and if you accomplish the task you shall have my daughter as a reward."

So the Prince began his labours, and he dug and shovelled without ceasing. On the seventh day, when he saw how little he had done, he became very sad, and gave up all hope. But in the evening the Fox appeared and said, "You do not deserve any help from me, but lie down and go to sleep. I will do the work." In the morning when he woke and looked out of the window, the mountain had disappeared.

Filled with joy, the Prince hurried to the King and told

him that his condition was fulfilled, and, whether he liked it or not, he must keep his word and give him his daughter.

So they both went away together, and before long the faithful Fox joined them.

"You certainly have got the best thing of all," said he. "But to the maiden of the golden palace the Golden Horse belongs."

"How am I to get it?" asked the Prince.

"Oh! I will tell you that," answered the Fox. "First take the beautiful maiden to the King who sent you to the golden palace. There will be great joy when you appear, and they will bring out the Golden Horse to you. Mount it at once, and shake hands with everybody, last of all with the beautiful maiden. When you have taken her hand firmly, pull her up beside you with a swing and gallop away. No one will be able to catch you, for the horse goes faster than the wind."

All this was successfully done, and the Prince carried off the beautiful maiden on the Golden Horse.

The Fox was not far off, and he said to the Prince, "Now I will help you to get the Golden Bird, too. When you approach the castle where the Golden Bird lives, let the maiden dismount, and I will take care of her. Then ride with the Golden Horse into the courtyard of the castle. There will be great rejoicing when they see you, and they will bring out the Golden Bird to you. As soon as you have the cage in your hand, gallop back to us and take up the maiden again."

When these plans had succeeded, and the Prince was ready to ride on with all his treasures, the Fox said to him:

"Now you must reward me for my help."

"What do you want?" asked the Prince.

"When you reach that wood, shoot me."

"That would indeed be gratitude!" said the Prince. "I can't possibly promise to do such a thing."

The Fox said, "If you won't do it, I must leave you; but before I go I will give you one more piece of advice. Beware of two things—buy no gallows-birds, and don't sit on the edge of a well." Saying which he ran off into the wood.

The Prince thought, "That is a strange animal; what whims he has. Who on earth would want to buy gallows-birds! And the desire to sit on the edge of a well has never yet seized me!"

He rode on with the beautiful maiden, and the road led him through the village where his two brothers had stayed behind. There was a great hubbub in the village, and when he asked what it was about, he was told that two persons were about to be hanged. When he got nearer he saw that they were his two brothers, who had wasted their goods, and committed all sorts of evil deeds. He asked if they could not be set free.

"If you ransom them," answered the people. "But why will you throw your money away in buying off these two wicked people?"

He did not stop to reflect, however, but paid the ransom for them, and when they were set free they all journeyed on together.

They came to the wood where they had first met the Fox. It was deliciously cool there, while the sun was broiling outside, so the two brothers said, "Let us sit down here by the well to rest a little and take some refreshment." The Prince agreed, and during the conversation he forgot what he was about, and, never dreaming of any foul play, seated himself on the edge of the well. But his two brothers threw him backwards into it, and went home to their father, taking with them the maiden, the Horse, and the Bird.

"Here we bring you not only the Golden Bird, but the Golden Horse, and the maiden from the golden palace, as our booty."

Thereupon there was great rejoicing. But the Horse would not eat, the Bird would not sing, and the maiden sat and wept all day.

The youngest brother had not perished, however. Happily the well was dry, and he fell upon soft moss without taking any harm; only, he could not get out.

Even in this great strait the faithful Fox did not forsake him, but came leaping down and scolded him for not taking his advice. "I can't leave you to your fate, though. I must help you to get back to the light of day." He told him to take tight hold of his tail, and then he dragged him up. "You are not out of every danger even now," said the Fox. "Your brothers were not sure of your death, so they have set watchers all over the wood to kill you if they see you."

A poor old man was sitting by the roadside, and the Prince exchanged clothes with him, and by this means he succeeded in reaching the King's court.

Nobody recognized him, but the Bird began to sing, the Horse began to eat, and the beautiful maiden left off crying.

In astonishment the King asked, "What does all this mean?"

The maiden answered: "I do not know; but I was very sad, and now I am gay. It seems to me that my true bridegroom must have come."

She told the King all that had happened, although the two brothers had threatened her with death if she betrayed anything. The King ordered every person in the palace to be brought before him. Among them came the Prince disguised as an old man in all his rags; but the maiden knew him at once, and fell on his neck. The wicked brothers were seized and executed. But the Prince was married to the beautiful maiden, and proclaimed heir to the King.

But what became of the poor Fox? Long afterwards, when the Prince went out into the fields one day, he met the Fox, who said: "You have everything that you can desire, but there is no end to my misery. It still lies in your power to release me." And again he implored the Prince to shoot him.

At last the Prince consented to do as he was asked, and no sooner was it done than the Fox was changed into a man; no other than the brother of the beautiful princess, at last set free from the evil spell which so long had lain upon him.

There was nothing now wanting to their happiness for the rest of their lives.

THE WOLF AND THE SEVEN KIDS

THERE was once an old Nanny-goat who had seven Kids, and she was just as fond of them as a mother of her children. One day she was going into the woods to fetch some food for them, so she called them all up to her, and said:

"My dear children, I am going out into the woods. Beware of the Wolf! If once he gets into the house, he will eat you up. The rascal often disguises himself, but you will know him by his rough voice and his black feet."

The Kids said, "Oh, we will be very careful, dear mother. You may be quite happy about us."

Bleating tenderly, the old Goat went off to her work. Before long, someone knocked at the door, and cried:

"Open the door, dear children! Your mother has come back and brought something for each of you."

But the Kids knew quite well by the voice that it was the Wolf.

"We won't open the door," they cried. "You are not our mother. She has a soft gentle voice. But yours is rough, and we are quite sure that you are the Wolf."

So he went away to a shop and bought a lump of chalk, which he ate, and it made his voice quite soft. He went back, knocked at the door again, and cried:

"Open the door, dear children. Your mother has come back and brought something for each of you."

But the Wolf had put one of his paws on the window sill, where the Kids saw it, and cried:

"We won't open the door. Our mother has not got a black foot as you have. You are the Wolf."

Then the Wolf ran to a Baker, and said, "I have bruised my foot; please put some dough on it." And when the Baker had put some dough on his foot, he ran to the Miller and said, "Strew some flour on my foot."

The Miller thought, "The old Wolf is going to take somebody in," and refused.

But the Wolf said, "If you don't do it, I will eat you up."

So the Miller was frightened, and whitened his paws. People are like that, you know.

Now the wretch went for the third time to the door, and knocked, and said:

"Open the door, children. Your dear mother has come home, and has brought something for each of you out of the wood."

The Kids cried, "Show us your feet first, that we may be sure you are our mother."

He put his paws on the window sill, and when they saw that they were white, they believed all he said, and opened the door.

Alas! It was the Wolf who walked in. They were terrified, and tried to hide themselves. One ran under the table, the second jumped into bed, the third into the oven, the fourth ran into the kitchen, the fifth got into the cupboard, the sixth into the wash-tub, and the seventh hid in the tall clock-case. But the Wolf found them all but one, and made short work of them. He swallowed one after the other, except the youngest one in the clock-case, whom he did not find. When he had satisfied his appetite, he took himself off, and lay down in a meadow outside, where he soon fell asleep.

Not long after the old Nanny-goat came back from the woods. Oh! What a terrible sight met her eyes! The house door was wide open, table, chairs, and benches were overturned, the washing bowl was smashed to atoms, the covers and pillows torn from the bed. She searched all over the house for her children, but nowhere were they to be found. She called them by name, one by one, but no one answered. At last, when she came to the youngest, a tiny voice cried:

"I am here, dear mother, hidden in the clock-case."

She brought him out, and he told her that the Wolf had come and devoured all the others.

You may imagine how she wept over her children.

At last, in her grief, she went out, and the youngest Kid ran by her side. When they went into the meadow, there lay the Wolf under a tree, making the branches shake with his snores. They examined him from every side, and they could plainly see movements within his distended body.

"Ah, heavens!" thought the Goat, "is it possible that my poor children, whom he ate for his supper, should be still alive?"

She sent the Kid running to the house to fetch scissors, needles, and thread. Then she cut a hole in the monster's side, and, hardly had she begun, when a Kid popped out its head. As soon as the hole was big enough, all six jumped out, one after the other, all alive, and without having suffered the least injury, for, in his greed, the monster had swallowed them whole. You may imagine the mother's joy. She hugged them, and skipped about like a tailor on his wedding day. At last she said:

"Go and fetch some big stones, children, and we will fill up the brute's body while he is asleep."

Then the seven Kids brought a lot of stones, as fast as they could carry them, and stuffed the Wolf with them till he could hold no more. The old mother quickly sewed him up, without his having noticed anything, or even moved.

At last, when the Wolf got up, the stones made him feel very thirsty, and he wanted to go to a spring to drink. But as soon as he moved, the stones began to roll about and rattle inside him. Then he cried:

> "What's the rumbling and tumbling
> That sets my stomach grumbling?
> I thought 'twas six Kids, flesh and bones,
> Now find it's naught but rolling stones."

When he reached the spring, and stooped over the water to drink, the heavy stones dragged him down, and he was drowned.

When the seven Kids saw what had happened, they came running up, and cried aloud: "The Wolf is dead, the Wolf is dead!" And they and their mother capered and danced round the spring in their joy.

TOM THUMB

A poor Peasant sat one evening by his hearth and poked the fire, while his Wife sat opposite spinning. He said: "What a sad thing it is that we have no children. Our home is so quiet, while other folk's houses are noisy and cheerful."

"Yes," answered his Wife, and she sighed: "Even if it were an only one, and if it were no bigger than my thumb, I should be quite content. We would love it with all our hearts."

Now, some time after this, she had a little boy who was strong and healthy, but was no bigger than a thumb. Then they said: "Well, our wish is fulfilled, and, small as he is, we will love him dearly."

Because of his tiny stature they called him Tom Thumb. They let him want for nothing, yet the child grew no bigger, but remained the same size as when he was born. Still, he looked out on the world with intelligent eyes, and soon showed himself a clever and agile creature, who was lucky in all he attempted.

One day, when the Peasant was preparing to go into the forest to cut wood, he said to himself: "I wish I had someone to bring the cart after me."

"Oh, Father!" said Tom Thumb, "I will soon bring it. You leave it to me. It shall be there at the appointed time."

Then the Peasant laughed, and said: "How can that be? You are much too small even to hold the reins."

"That doesn't matter, if only Mother will harness the horse," answered Tom. "I will sit in his ear and tell him where to go."

"Very well," said the Father, "we will try it for once."

When the time came, the Mother harnessed the horse, set Tom in his ear, and then the little creature called out "Gee-up" and "Whoa" in turn, and directed it where to go. It went quite well, just as though it were being driven by its master; and they went the right way to the wood. Now it happened that while the cart was turning a corner, and Tom was calling to the horse, two strange men appeared on the scene.

"My goodness," said one, "what is this? There goes a cart, and a driver is calling to the horse, but there is nothing to be seen."

"There is something queer about this," said the other. "We will follow the cart and see where it stops."

The cart went on deep into the forest, and arrived quite safely at the place where the wood was cut.

When Tom spied his Father, he said: "You see, Father, here I am with the cart; now lift me down." The Father held the horse with his left hand, and took his little son out of its ear with the right. Then Tom sat down quite happily on a straw.

When the two strangers noticed him, they did not know what to say for astonishment.

Then one drew the other aside, and said: "Listen, that little creature might make our fortune if we were to show him in the town for money. We will buy him."

So they went up to the Peasant, and said: "Sell us the little man; he shall be well looked after with us."

"No," said the Peasant; "he is the delight of my eyes, and I will not sell him for all the gold in the world."

But Tom Thumb, when he heard the bargain, crept up by the folds of his Father's coat, placed himself on his shoulder, and whispered in his ear: "Father, let me go; I will soon come back again."

Then his Father gave him to the two men for a fine piece of gold.

"Where will you sit?" they asked him.

"Oh, put me on the brim of your hat, then I can walk up and down and observe the neighbourhood without falling down."

They did as he wished, and when Tom had said good-bye to his Father, they went away with him.

They walked on till it was twilight, when the little man said: "You must lift me down."

"Stay where you are," answered the Man on whose head he sat.

"No," said Tom, "I will come down. Lift me down immediately."

The Man took his hat off and set the little creature in a field by the wayside. He jumped and crept about for a time, here and there among the sods, then slipped suddenly into a mouse-hole which he had discovered.

"Good evening, gentlemen, just you go home without me," he called out to them in mockery.

They ran about and poked with sticks into the mouse-hole, but all in vain. Tom crept further and further back, and, as it soon got quite dark, they were forced to go home, full of anger, and with empty purses.

When Tom noticed that they were gone, he crept out of his underground hiding-place again. "It is dangerous walking in this field in the dark," he said. "One might easily break one's leg or one's neck." Luckily, he came to an empty snail shell. "Thank goodness," he said. "I can pass the night in safety here," and he sat down.

Not long after, just when he was about to go to sleep, he heard two men pass by. One said: "How shall we set about stealing the rich parson's gold and silver?"

"I can tell you," interrupted Tom.

"What was that?" said one robber in a fright. "I heard someone speak."

They remained standing and listened.

Then Tom spoke again: "Take me with you and I will help you."

"Where are you?" they asked.

"Just look on the ground and see where the voice comes from," he answered.

At last the thieves found him, and lifted him up. "You little urchin, are *you* going to help us?"

"Yes," he said; "I will creep between the iron bars in the pastor's room, and will hand out to you what you want."

"All right," they said, "we will see what you can do."

When they came to the parsonage, Tom crept into the room, but called out immediately with all his strength to the others: "Do you want everything that is here?"

The thieves were frightened, and said: "Do speak softly, and don't wake anyone."

But Tom pretended not to understand, and called out again: "What do you want? Everything?"

The Cook, who slept above, heard him and sat up in bed and listened. But the thieves were so frightened that they retreated a little way. At last they summoned up courage again, and thought to themselves, "The little rogue wants to tease us." So they came back and whispered to him: "Now, do be serious, and hand us something."

Then Tom called out again, as loud as he could, "I will give you everything if only you will hold out your hands."

The Maid, who was listening intently, heard him quite distinctly, jumped out of bed, and stumbled to the door. The thieves turned and fled, running as though wild huntsmen were after them. But the Maid, seeing nothing, went to get a light. When she came back with it, Tom without being seen, slipped out into the barn. The Maid, after she had searched every corner and found nothing, went to bed again, thinking she had been dreaming with her eyes and ears open.

Tom Thumb climbed about in the hay, and found a splendid place to sleep. There he determined to rest till day came, and then to go home to his parents. But he had other experiences to go through first. This world is full of trouble and sorrow!

The Maid got up in the grey dawn to feed the cows. First she went into the barn, where she piled up an armful of hay, the very bundle in which poor Tom was asleep. But he slept so soundly that he knew nothing till he was almost in the mouth of the cow, who was eating him up with the hay.

"Heavens!" he said, "how did I get into this mill?" But he soon saw where he was, and the great thing was to avoid being crushed between the cow's teeth. At last, whether he liked it or not, he had to go down the cow's throat.

"The windows have been forgotten in this house," he said. "The sun does not shine into it, and no light has been provided."

Altogether he was very ill pleased with his quarters, and, worst of all, more and more hay came in at the door, and the space grew narrower and narrower. At last he called out, in his fear, as loud as he could, "Don't give me any more food. Don't give me any more food."

The Maid was just milking the cow, and when she heard the same voice as in the night, without seeing any-one, she was frightened, and slipped from her stool and spilled the milk. Then, in the greatest haste, she ran to her master, and said: "Oh, your Reverence, the cow has spoken!"

"You are mad," he answered. But he went into the stable himself to see what was happening.

Scarcely had he set foot in the cow-shed before Tom began again, "Don't bring me any more food."

Then the Pastor was terrified too, and thought that the cow must be bewitched; so he ordered it to be killed. It was slaughtered accordingly, but the stomach, in which Tom was hidden, was thrown into a haystack. Tom had the greatest trouble in working his way out. Just as he stuck out his head, a hungry Wolf ran by and snapped up the whole stomach with one bite. But still Tom did not lose courage. "Perhaps the Wolf will listen to reason," he said. So he called out, "Dear Wolf, I know where you can find a magnificent meal."

"Where is it to be had?" asked the Wolf.

"Why, in such and such a house," answered Tom. "You must squeeze through the grating of the store-room window, and there you will find cakes, bacon, and sausages, as many as you can possibly eat"; and he went on to describe his father's house.

The Wolf did not wait to hear this twice, and at night forced himself in through the grating, and ate to his heart's content. When he was satisfied, he wanted to go away again. But he had grown so fat that he could not get out the same way. Tom had reckoned on this, and began to make a great commotion inside the Wolf's body, struggling and screaming with all his might.

"Be quiet," said the Wolf. "You will wake up the people of the house."

"All very fine," answered Tom. "You have eaten your fill, and now I am going to make merry." And he began to scream again with all his might.

At last his father and mother woke up, ran to the room, and looked through the crack of the door. When they saw a Wolf, they went away, and the husband fetched his axe, and the wife a scythe.

"You stay behind," said the man, as they came into the room. "If my blow does not kill him, you must attack him with the scythe."

When Tom Thumb heard his Father's voice, he called out: "Dear Father, I am here, inside the Wolf's body."

Full of joy, his Father cried, "Heaven be praised! our dear child is found again," and he bade his wife throw aside the scythe that it might not injure Tom.

Then he gathered himself together, and struck the

Wolf a blow on the head, so that it fell down lifeless. Then they opened up the body, and took their little boy out.

"Ah," said his Father, "what trouble we have been in about you."

"Yes, Father, I have travelled about the world, and I am thankful to breathe fresh air again."

"Wherever have you been?" they asked.

"In a Mouse's hole, a Cow's stomach, and a Wolf's maw," he answered. "And now I shall stay with you."

"And we will never sell you again, for all the riches in the world," they said, kissing and fondling their dear child.

Then they gave him food and drink, and had new clothes made for him, as his own had been spoiled in his travels.

THE WREN AND THE BEAR

ONCE upon a time, in the summer, a Bear and a Wolf were taking a walk in the woods when the Bear heard a bird singing most beautifully. "Brother Wolf, what kind of bird is that singing so beautifully?" he asked.

"That is the King of the birds, and we must make obeisance to it."

But it was really a Wren.

"If that is so," said the Bear, "I should like to see his royal palace. Come, you must take me to it."

"That's not so easy," said the Wolf. "You must wait till the Queen comes."

Soon after the Queen made her appearance, bringing food in her beak, and the King came with her to feed their young. The Bear would have liked to go in at once, but the Wolf held him by the sleeve, and said, "No, now you must wait till the King and Queen fly away again."

So they marked the opening of the nest, and trudged on. But the Bear had no rest till he could see the royal palace, and before long he went back.

The King and the Queen had gone out again. He peeped in, and saw five or six young ones lying in the nest.

"Is that the royal palace?" cried the Bear. "What a miserable place! And do you mean to say that you are royal children? You must be changelings!"

When the young Wrens heard this, they were furious, and shrieked, "No, indeed we're not. Our parents are honest people. We must have this out with you."

The Bear and the Wolf were very much frightened. They turned round and ran home to their dens.

But the young Wrens continued to shriek and scream aloud. And when their parents came back with more food, they said, "We won't touch as much as the leg of a fly, even if we starve, till you tell us whether we are really your lawful children or not. The Bear has been here calling us names."

Then said the old King, "Only be quiet, and this shall be seen to."

Thereupon he and his wife the Queen flew off to the Bear in his den, and called in to him, "Old Bruin, why have you been calling our children names? It will turn out badly for you, and it will lead to a bloody war between us."

So war was declared, and all the four-footed animals were called together—the ox, the ass, the cow, the stag, the roedeer, and every other creature on the earth.

But the Wren called together every creature that flew

in the air, not only birds both large and small, but also the gnats, the hornets, the bees, and the flies.

When the time came for the war to begin, the Wren sent out scouts to discover where the commanding generals of the enemy were to be found. The gnats were the most cunning of all. They swarmed in the woods where the enemy was assembled, and at last they hid themselves under a leaf of the tree where the orders were being given.

The Bear called the Fox up to him and said, "You are the slyest of all the animals, Reynard. You shall be our general, and lead us."

"Very good," said the Fox; "but what shall we have for a signal?" But nobody could think of anything. Then said the Fox, "I have a fine, long, bushy tail, which almost looks like a red feather brush. When I hold my tail erect, things are going well, and you must march forward at once; but if it droops, you must all run away as hard as ever you can."

When the gnats heard this they flew straight home and told the Wrens every detail.

When the day broke, all the four-footed animals came rushing to the spot where the battle was to take place. They came with such a clatter that the earth shook.

The Wren and his army also came swarming through the air. They fluttered and buzzed enough to terrify one, and then they made for one another.

The Wren sent the Hornet down with orders to seat

189

herself under the tail of the Fox, and to sting him with all her might.

When the Fox felt the first sting he quivered, and raised one leg in the air; but he bore it bravely, and kept his tail erect. At the second sting he was forced to let it droop for a moment, but the third time he could bear it no longer. He screamed, and down went his tail between his legs. When the animals saw this they thought all was lost, and off they ran as fast as they could run, each to his own den.

So the birds won the battle.

When it was over the King and the Queen flew home to their children, and cried, "Children, be happy! Eat and drink to your hearts' content; we have won the battle."

But the young Wrens said, "We won't eat till the Bear comes here to make an apology, and says that we are really and truly your lawful children."

The Wren flew to the Bear's den, and cried, "Old Bruin, you will have to come and apologise to my children for calling them names, or else you will have all your ribs broken."

So in great terror the Bear crept to the nest and apologised, and at last the young Wrens were satisfied, and they ate and drank and made merry till far into the night.

THE WATER OF LIFE

THERE was once a King who was so ill that it was thought impossible to save his life. He had three sons, and they were all in great distress on his account, and they went into the castle gardens and wept at the thought that he must die. An old man came up to them and asked the cause of their grief. They told him that their father was dying, and nothing could save him. The old man said, "There is only one remedy which I know; it is the Water of Life. If he drinks of it, he will recover, but it is very difficult to find."

The eldest son said, "I will soon find it." And he went to the sick man to ask permission to go in search of the Water of Life, as that was the only thing to cure him.

"No," said the King. "The danger is too great. I would rather die."

But he persisted so long that at last the King gave his permission.

The Prince thought, "If I bring this water I shall be the favourite, and I shall inherit the kingdom."

So he set off, and when he had ridden some distance he came upon a Dwarf standing on the road, who cried, "Whither away so fast?"

"Stupid little fellow," said the Prince, proudly. "What business is it of yours?" and rode on.

The little man was very angry, and made an evil vow.

Soon after, the Prince came to a gorge in the mountains, and the further he rode the narrower it became, till he could go no further. His horse could neither go forward nor turn round for him to dismount; so there he sat, jammed in.

The sick King waited a long time for him, but he never came back. Then the second son said, "Father, let me go and find the Water of Life," thinking, "if my brother is dead I shall have the kingdom."

The King at first refused to let him go, but at last he gave his consent. So the Prince started on the same road as his brother, and met the same Dwarf, who stopped him and asked where he was going in such a hurry.

"What does it matter to you?" he said, and rode away without looking back.

But the Dwarf cast a spell over him, and he, too, got into a narrow gorge like his brother, where he could go neither backwards nor forwards.

This is what happens to the haughty.

As the second son also stayed away, the youngest one offered to go and fetch the Water of Life, and at last the King was obliged to let him go.

When he met the Dwarf, and he asked him where he was hurrying to, he stopped and said, "I am searching for the Water of Life, because my father is dying."

"Do you know where it is to be found?"

"No," said the Prince.

"As you have spoken pleasantly to me, and not been haughty like your false brothers, I will help you and tell you how to find the Water of Life. It flows from a fountain in the courtyard of an enchanted castle. But you will never get in unless I give you an iron rod and two loaves of bread. With the rod strike three times on the iron gate of the castle, and it will spring open. Inside you will find two Lions with wide-open jaws, but if you throw a loaf to each they will be quiet. Then you must make haste to fetch the Water of Life before it strikes twelve, or the gates of the castle will close and you will be shut in."

The Prince thanked him, took the rod and the loaves, and set off. When he reached the castle all was just as the Dwarf had said. At the third knock the gate flew open, and when he had pacified the Lions with the loaves, he walked into the castle. In the great hall he found several enchanted Princes, and he took the rings from their fingers. He also took a sword and a loaf, which were lying by them. On passing into the next room he found a beautiful Maiden, who rejoiced at his coming. She embraced him, and said that he had saved her, and should have the whole of her kingdom; and if he would come back in a year she would marry him. She also told him where to find the fountain with the enchanted water; but, she said, he must make haste to get out of the castle before the clock struck twelve.

Then he went on, and came to a room where there was a beautiful bed freshly made, and as he was very tired he thought he would take a little rest; so he lay down and fell asleep. When he woke it was striking a quarter to twelve. He sprang up in a fright, and ran to the fountain, and took some of the water in a cup which was lying near, and then hurried away. The clock struck just as he reached the iron gate, and it banged so quickly that it took off a bit of his heel.

He was rejoiced at having got some of the Water of Life, and hastened on his homeward journey. He again passed the Dwarf, who, when he saw the sword and the loaf, said, "Those things will be of much service to you. You will be able to strike down whole armies with the sword, and the loaf will never come to an end."

The Prince did not want to go home without his brothers, and he said, "Good Dwarf, can you not tell me where my brothers are? They went in search of the Water of Life before I did, but they never came back."

"They are both stuck fast in a narrow mountain gorge. I cast a spell over them because of their pride."

Then the Prince begged so hard that they might be released that at last the Dwarf yielded; but he warned him against them, and said, "Beware of them; they have bad hearts."

He was delighted to see his brothers when they came back, and told them all that had happened to him; how he had found the Water of Life, and brought a goblet full with him. How he had released a beautiful Princess, who would wait a year for him and then marry him, and he would become a great Prince.

Then they rode away together, and came to a land where famine and war were raging. The King thought he would be utterly ruined, so great was the destitution.

The Prince went to him and gave him the loaf, and with it he fed and satisfied his whole kingdom. The Prince also gave him his sword, and he smote the whole army of his enemies with it, and then he was able to live in peace and quiet. Then the Prince took back his sword and his loaf, and the three brothers rode on. But they had to pass through two more countries where war and famine were raging, and each time the Prince gave his sword and his loaf to the King, and in this way he saved three kingdoms.

After that they took a ship and crossed the sea. During the passage the two elder brothers said to each other, "Our youngest brother found the Water of Life, and we did not, so our father will give him the kingdom which we ought to have, and he will take away the luck from us."

This thought made them very vindictive, and they made up their minds to get rid of him. They waited till he was asleep, and then they emptied the Water of Life from his goblet and took it themselves, and filled up his cup with salt sea water.

As soon as they got home the youngest Prince took his goblet to the King, so that he might drink of the water which was to make him well; but after drinking only a few drops of the sea-water he became more ill than ever. As he was bewailing himself, his two elder sons came to him and accused the youngest of trying to poison him, and said that they had the real Water of Life, and gave him some. No sooner had he drunk it than he felt better, and he soon became as strong and well as he had been in his youth.

Then the two went to their youngest brother, and mocked him, saying, "It was you who found the Water of Life; you had all the trouble, while we have the reward. You should have been wiser, and kept your eyes open; we stole it from you while you were asleep on the ship. When the end of the year comes, one of us will go and bring away the beautiful Princess. But don't dare to betray us. Our father will certainly not believe you, and if you say a single word you will lose your life. Your only chance is to keep silent."

The old King was very angry with his youngest son, thinking that he had tried to take his life. So he had the Court assembled to give judgment upon him, and it was decided that he must be secretly got out of the way.

One day when the Prince was going out hunting, thinking no evil, the King's Huntsman was ordered to go with him. Seeing the Huntsman look sad, the Prince said to him, "My good Huntsman, what is the matter with you?"

The Huntsman answered, "I can't bear to tell you, and yet I must."

The Prince said, "Say it out; whatever it is I will forgive you."

"Alas!" said the Huntsman, "I am to shoot you; it is the King's command."

The Prince was horror-stricken, and said, "Dear Huntsman, do not kill me, give me my life. Let me have your dress, and you shall have my royal robes."

The Huntsman said, "I will gladly do so; I could never have shot you." So they changed clothes, and the Huntsman went home, but the Prince wandered away into the forest.

After a time three wagon loads of gold and precious stones came to the King for his youngest son. They were sent by the Kings who had been saved by the Prince's sword and his miraculous loaf, and who now wished to show their gratitude.

Then the old King thought, "What if my son really was innocent?" and said to his people, "If only he were still alive! How sorry I am that I ordered him to be killed."

"He is still alive," said the Huntsman. "I could not find it in my heart to carry out your commands," and he told the King what had taken place.

A load fell from the King's heart on hearing the good

news, and he sent out a proclamation to all parts of his kingdom that his son was to come home, where he would be received with great favour.

In the meantime, the Princess had caused a road to be made of pure shining gold leading to her castle, and told her people that whoever came riding straight along it would be the true bridegroom, and they were to admit him. But anyone who came either on one side of the road or the other would not be the right one, and he was not to be let in.

When the year had almost passed, the eldest Prince thought that he would hurry to the Princess, and by giving himself out as her deliverer would gain a wife and a kingdom as well. So he rode away, and when he saw the beautiful golden road he thought it would be a thousand pities to ride upon it; so he turned aside, and rode to the right of it. But when he reached the gate the people told him that he was not the true bridegroom, and he had to go away.

Soon after the second Prince came, and when he saw the golden road he thought it would be a thousand pities for his horse to tread upon it; so he turned aside, and rode on the left of it. But when he reached the gate he was also told that he was not the true bridegroom, and, like his brother, was turned away.

When the year had quite come to an end, the third Prince came out of the wood to ride to his beloved, and through her to forget all his past sorrows. So on he went,

thinking only of her, and wishing to be with her; and he
never even saw the golden road. His horse cantered right
along the middle of it, and when he reached the gate it
was flung open and the Princess received him joyfully,
and called him her Deliverer, and the Lord of her Kingdom. Their marriage was celebrated without delay, and
with much rejoicing. When it was over, she told him that
his father had called him back and forgiven him. So he
went to him and told him everything; how his brothers
had deceived him, and how they had forced him to keep
silence. The old King wanted to punish them, but they
had taken a ship and sailed away over the sea, and they
never came back as long as they lived.

JORINDA AND JORINGEL

THERE was once an old castle in the middle of a vast thick woods. In it there lived an old woman who was a witch. By day she made herself into a cat or a screech-owl, but at night she regularly became a human being again. In this way she was able to decoy wild beasts and birds, which she would kill and boil, or roast. If any man came within a hundred paces of the castle, he was forced to stand still and could not move from the place till she gave the word of release. But if a maiden came within the circle she changed her into a bird, and shut her up in a cage which she carried into a room in the castle. She

must have had seven thousand cages of this kind, containing pretty birds in the castle.

Now, there was once a maiden who was called Jorinda, and she was more beautiful than all other maidens. She had promised to marry a very handsome young man named Joringel. They were in their courting days, and took the greatest delight in one another's company. One day they went for a walk in a wood to talk quietly to each other. "Take care," said Joringel; "do not go so near the castle." It was a lovely evening. The sunshine glanced between the tree-trunks of the dark green wood, and the turtle-doves sang plaintively on the old beech-trees. Jorinda sat down in the sunshine, from time to time weeping and bewailing herself, while Joringel joined in her lamentation. They were as miserable as if they had been going to die. They looked round; they had lost their way, and did not know in what direction to turn to get home. Half the sun appeared above the mountain; half had sunk below. Joringel looked into the thicket, and saw the old walls of the castle quite close to them. He was terror-struck, and almost died of fright. Jorinda was singing:

> *"My birdie with its ring so red*
> *Sings sorrow, sorrow, sorrow;*
> *My love will mourn when I am dead,*
> *Tomorrow, morrow, mor——jug, jug."*

Joringel looked at her, but she was changed into a nightingale who sang "Jug, jug."

A screech-owl with glowing eyes flew three times round her, and cried three times "Shu hu-hu." Joringel could not stir. He stood like a stone without being able to speak, or cry, or move hand or foot. The sun had now set. The owl flew into a bush, out of which appeared almost at the same moment a crooked old woman, skinny and yellow. She had big, red eyes and a crooked nose, whose tip reached her chin. She mumbled something, caught the nightingale, and carried it away in her hand. Joringel could not say a word nor move from the spot, and the nightingale was gone. At last the old woman came back, and said in a droning voice: "Greeting to thee, Zachiel! When the moon shines upon the cage unloose the captive, Zachiel!"

Then Joringel was free. He fell on his knees before the witch, and implored her to give back his Jorinda. But she said he should never have her again, and went away. He pleaded, he wept, he lamented, but all in vain. "Alas! What is to become of me?" said Joringel. At last he went away, and arrived at a strange village, where he spent a long time in keeping sheep. He often wandered round about the castle, but did not go too near it. At last he dreamt one night that he found a blood-red flower, in the midst of which was a beautiful large pearl, He plucked the flower, and took it to the castle. Whatever he touched with it was made free of enchantment. He dreamt, too, that by this means he had found his Jorinda again. In the morning when he awoke he began to search over hill and dale, in the hope of finding a flower like this. He searched till the ninth day, when he found the flower early in the morning. In the middle was a big dew-drop, as big as the finest pearl. This flower he carried day and night, till he reached the castle. He was not held fast as before when he came within the hundred paces of the castle, but walked straight up to the door.

Joringel was filled with joy; he touched the door with the flower, and it flew open. He went in through the court, and listened for the sound of birds. He went on, and found the hall, where the witch was feeding the birds in the seven thousand cages. When she saw Joringel she was angry, very angry—scolded, and spat poison and gall at him. He paid no attention to her, but turned away and scanned the bird-cages. Yes, but there were many hundred nightingales. How was he to find his Jorinda?

While he was looking about in this way he noticed that the old woman was secretly removing a cage with a bird inside, and was making for the door. He sprang swiftly towards her, touched the cage and the witch with the flower. Now the witch no longer had the power to exercise her spells. Jorinda stood there, as beautiful as before, and threw her arms around Joringel's neck. Then he changed all the other birds back into maidens again, and went home with Jorinda, and they lived long and happily together.

THE GOOSEGIRL

THERE was once an old Queen whose husband had been dead for many years, and she had a very beautiful daughter. When she grew up she was betrothed to a Prince in a distant country. When the time came for the maiden to be married, the old Queen packed up quantities of clothes and jewels, gold and silver, cups and ornaments, and, in fact, everything suitable to a royal outfit, for she loved her daughter very dearly.

She also sent a Waiting-woman to travel with her, and to put her hand into that of the bridegroom. They each had a horse. The Princess's horse was called Falada, and it could speak.

When the hour of departure came, the old Queen went to her bedroom, and with a needle pricked her finger and made it bleed. Then she held a piece of white cloth under it, and let three drops of blood fall on to it. This cloth she gave to her daughter, and said, "Dear child, take good care of this. It will stand you in good stead on the journey." They then bade each other a sorrowful farewell. The Princess hid the cloth in her bosom, mounted her horse, and set out to her bridegroom's country.

When they had ridden for a time the Princess became very thirsty, and said to the Waiting-woman, "Please fetch me some water, in my cup from the stream. I would like something to drink."

"If you are thirsty," said the Waiting-woman, "dismount yourself, lie down by the water, and drink. I don't choose to be your servant."

So, in her great thirst, the Princess dismounted, stooped down to the stream and drank, for she might not have her golden cup. The poor Princess said, "Alas!" and the drops of blood answered, "If your mother knew this it would break her heart."

The royal bride was humble, so she said nothing, but mounted her horse again. Then they rode several miles further. But the day was warm, the sun was scorching, and the Princess was soon thirsty again.

When they reached a river she called out again to her

Waiting-woman, "Please give me some water in my golden cup!"

She had forgotten all about the rude words which had been said to her. But the Waiting-woman answered more haughtily than ever, "If you want water to drink, get the water for yourself. I won't be your servant."

Being very thirsty, the Princess dismounted, and knelt by the flowing water. She cried, and said, "Ah me!" and the drops of blood answered, "If your mother knew this it would break her heart."

While she stooped over the water to drink, the piece of cloth with the drops of blood on it fell out of her bosom, and floated away on the stream; but she never noticed this in her great fear. The Waiting-woman, however, had seen it, and rejoiced at getting more power over the bride. By losing the drops of blood the Princess had become weak and powerless.

Now, when she was about to mount her horse Falada again, the Waiting-woman said, "By rights, Falada belongs to me; this jade will do for you!"

The poor little Princess was obliged to give way. Then the Waiting-woman, in a harsh voice ordered her to take off her royal robes, and to put on her own mean garments. Finally, she forced her to swear before heaven that she would not tell a creature at the Court what had taken place. Had she not taken the oath she would have been killed on the spot. But Falada saw all this and marked it.

The Waiting-woman then mounted Falada and put the

real bride on her poor jade, and they continued their journey.

There was great rejoicing when they arrived at the castle. The Prince hurried towards them, and lifted the Waiting-woman from her horse, thinking she was his bride. She was led upstairs, but the real Princess had to stay below.

The old King looked out of the window and saw the delicate, pretty, little creature standing in the courtyard. He went to the bridal apartments and asked the bride about her companion, who was left standing in the courtyard, and wished to know who she was.

"I picked her up on the way, and brought her with me for company. Give the girl something to do to keep her from idling."

But the old King had no work for her, and could not think of anything. At last he said, "I have a little lad who looks after the geese; she may help him."

The boy was called little Conrad, and the real bride was sent with him to look after the geese.

Soon after, the false bride said to the Prince, "Dear husband, I pray you do me a favour.'

He answered, "That will I gladly."

"Well, then, let the knacker be called to cut off the head of the horse I rode; it angered me on the way."

Really, she was afraid that the horse would speak, and tell of her treatment of the Princess. So it was settled, and the faithful Falada had to die.

When this came to the ear of the real Princess, she promised the knacker a piece of gold if he would do her a slight service. There was a great dark gateway to the town, through which she had to pass every morning and evening. "Would he place Falada's head in this gateway, so that she might see him as she passed?"

The knacker promised to do as she wished, and when the horse's head was struck off, he hung it up in the dark gateway. In the early morning, when she and Conrad went through the gateway, she said in passing:

"Alas! dear Falada, there thou hangest."

And the Head answered:

"Alas! Queen's daughter, there thou gangest.
If thy mother knew thy fate,
Her heart would break with grief so great."

Then they passed on out of the town, right into the fields, with the geese. When they reached the meadow, the Princess sat down on the grass, and let down her hair. It shone like pure gold, and when little Conrad saw it, he was so delighted that he wanted to pluck some out; but she said:

"Blow, blow, little breeze
And Conrad's hat seize.
Let him join in the chase
While away it is whirled,
Till my tresses are curled
And I rest in my place."

Then a strong wind sprang up, which blew away Conrad's hat right over the fields, and he had to run after it. When he came back, she had finished combing her hair, and it was all put up again; so he could not get a single hair. This made him very sulky, and he would not say another word to her. And they tended the geese till evening, when they went home.

Next morning, when they passed under the gateway, the Princess said:

> "Alas! dear Falada, there thou hangest."

Falada answered:

> "Alas! Queen's daughter, there thou gangest.
> If thy mother knew thy fate,
> Her heart would break with grief so great."

Again, when they reached the meadows, the Princess undid her hair and began combing it. Conrad ran to pluck some out; but she said quickly:

> "Blow, blow, little breeze,
> And Conrad's hat seize.
> Let him join in the chase
> While away it is whirled,
> Till my tresses are curled
> And I rest in my place."

The wind sprang up and blew Conrad's hat far away

over the fields, and he had to run after it. When he came back the hair was all put up again, and he could not pull a single hair out. And they tended the geese till the evening. When they got home Conrad went to the old King, and said, "I won't tend the geese with that maiden again."

"Why not?" asked the King.

"Oh, she vexes me every day."

The old King then ordered him to say what she did to vex him.

Conrad said, "In the morning, when we pass under the dark gateway with the geese, she talks to a horse's head which is hung up on the wall. She says:

> *'Alas! Falada, there thou hangest,'*

and the Head answers:

> *'Alas! Queen's daughter, there thou gangest.*
> *If thy mother knew thy fate,*
> *Her heart would break with grief so great.'"*

Then Conrad went on to tell the King all that happened in the meadow, and how he had to run after his hat.

The old King ordered Conrad to go out next day as usual. Then he placed himself behind the dark gateway, and heard the Princess speaking to Falada's head. He also followed her into the field, and hid himself behind a bush, and with his own eyes he saw the Goosegirl and the lad come driving the geese into the field. Then, after a time, he saw the girl let down her hair, which glittered in the sun. Directly after this, she said:

"Blow, blow, little breeze,
And Conrad's hat seize.
Let him join in the chase
While away it is whirled,
Till my tresses are curled
And I rest in my place."

Then came a puff of wind, which carried off Conrad's hat and he had to run after it. While he was away, the maiden combed and did up her hair; and all this the old King observed. Thereupon he went away unnoticed. In the evening, when the Goosegirl came home, he called her aside, and asked why she did all these things.

"That I may not tell you, nor may I tell any human creature. I have sworn it under the open sky, because if I had not done so I should have lost my life."

He pressed her sorely, and gave her no peace, but he could get nothing out of her. Then he said, "If you won't tell me, then tell your sorrows to the iron stove there," and he went away.

She crept up to the stove, and, beginning to weep and lament, unburdened her heart to it, and said: "Here I am, forsaken by all the world, and yet I am a Princess. A false Waiting-woman brought me to such a pass that I had to take off my royal robes. Then she took my place with my bridegroom, while I have to do mean service as a Goosegirl. If my mother knew it her heart would break."

The old King stood outside by the pipes of the stove, and heard all that she said. Then he came back, and told her to go away from the stove. He caused royal robes to be put upon her, and her beauty was a marvel. The old King called his son, and told him that he had a false bride —she was only a Waiting-woman; but the true bride was here, the so-called Goosegirl.

The young Prince was charmed with her youth and beauty. A great banquet was prepared, to which all the courtiers and good friends were bidden. The bridegroom sat at the head of the table, with the Princess on one side and the Waiting-woman at the other; but she was dazzled, and did not recognise the Princess in her brilliant apparel.

When they had eaten and drunk and were all very merry, the old King told everyone the true story about the Waiting-woman and the Princess. He ended by having the Waiting-woman banished from the country forever.

Then the young Prince married his true bride, and they ruled their kingdom together in peace and happiness.

THE TWELVE HUNTSMEN

THERE was once a Prince, who was betrothed to a Maiden whom he loved very much. One day when they were together, and very happy, a messenger came from the Prince's father, who was lying ill, to summon him home as he wished to see him before he died. He said to his beloved, "I must go away, and leave you now; but I give you this ring as a keepsake. When I am King, I will come and fetch you away."

Then he rode off, and when he got home he found his father on his death-bed. His father said, "My dear son, I wanted to see you once more before I die. Promise to marry the bride I have chosen for you," and he named a certain Princess.

His son was very sad and, without reflecting, promised to do what his father wished. Thereupon the King closed his eyes, and died.

Now, when the Prince had been proclaimed King, and the period of mourning was past, the time came when he had to keep his promise to his father. He made his offer to the Princess, and it was accepted. His betrothed heard of this, and grieved so much over his faithlessness that she very nearly died. Her father asked, "Dear child, why are you so sad? You shall have whatever you desire."

She thought for a moment, then said, "Dear Father, I want eleven maidens all exactly like me in face, figure, and height."

The King said, "If it is possible, your wish shall be fulfilled."

Then he caused a search to be made all over his kingdom, till the eleven maidens were found, all exactly like his daughter. The Princess ordered twelve huntsmen's dresses to be made, which she commanded the maidens to wear, putting on the twelfth herself. Then she took leave of her father, and rode away with the maidens to the court of her former bridegroom whom she loved so dearly. She asked him if he wanted any Huntsmen, and whether he would take them all into his service. The King did not recognise her, but, as they were all so handsome, he said that he would engage them. So they all entered the King's service.

Now, the King had a Lion which was a wonderful creature, for he knew all secret and hidden things. He said to the King one evening, "You fancy you have twelve Huntsmen there, don't you?"

"Yes," said the King.

"You are mistaken," said the Lion. "They are twelve maidens."

The King answered, "That can't be true! How can you prove it?"

"Oh, have some peas strewn in your anteroom tomorrow, and you will soon see. Men have a firm tread, and when they walk on peas they don't move. But maidens trip and trot and slide, and make the peas roll about."

The King was pleased with the Lion's advice, and ordered the peas to be strewn on the floor.

There was, however, a servant of the King who favoured the Huntsmen, and when he heard that they were to be put to this test, he went and told them all about it, and said, "The Lion is going to prove to the King that you are maidens."

The Princess thanked him, and said afterwards to her maidens, "Do your utmost to tread firmly on the peas."

Next morning, when the King ordered them to be called, they walked into the ante-chamber with so firm a tread that not a pea moved. When they had gone away, the King said to the Lion, "You lied; they walked just like men."

But the Lion answered, "They had been warned of the test, and were prepared for it. Just let twelve spinning-wheels be brought into the ante-chamber, and they will be delighted at the sight, as no man would be."

This plan also pleased the King, and he ordered the spinning-wheels. But again the kind servant warned the Huntsmen of the plan. When they were alone, the Princess said to her maidens, "Control yourselves, and don't so much as look at the spinning-wheels."

When the King next morning sent for the Huntsmen, they walked through the ante-chamber without even glancing at the spinning-wheels.

Then the King said to the Lion, "You lied to me. They *are* men; they never looked at the spinning-wheels."

The Lion answered, "They knew that they were on their trial, and restrained themselves."

But the King would not believe him any more.

The twelve Huntsmen always went with the King on his hunting expeditions, and the longer he had them, the better he liked them. Now, it happened one day when they were out hunting, that the news came of the royal bride's approach.

When the true bride heard it, the shock was so great that her heart nearly stopped, and she fell down in a dead faint. The King, thinking something had happened to his dear Huntsman, ran to help him, and pulled off his glove. Then he saw the ring which he had given to his first betrothed, and when he looked in her face he recognised her. He was so moved that he kissed her, and when she opened her eyes he said, "Thou are mine, and I am thine, and nobody in the world shall separate us."

Then he sent a messenger to the other bride, and begged her to go home, as he already had a wife. Their marriage was then celebrated, and the Lion was taken into favour again, as, after all, he had spoken the truth.

IRON HANS

THERE was once a King whose castle was surrounded by a forest full of game. One day he sent a Huntsman out to shoot a deer, but he never came back.

"Perhaps an accident has happened to him," said the King.

The next day he sent out two more Huntsmen to look for him, but they did not return either. On the third day he sent for all his Huntsmen, and said to them, "Search the whole forest without ceasing, until you have found all three."

But not a single man of all these, or one of the pack of hounds they took with them, ever came back. From this time forth no one would venture into the forest. There it lay, wrapped in silence and solitude, with only an occasional eagle or hawk circling over it.

This continued for several years, and then one day a strange Huntsman sought an audience with the King, and offered to penetrate into the dangerous wood. The King, however, would not give him permission, and said, "It's not safe, and I am afraid if you go in that you will never come out again, any more than all the others."

The Huntsman answered, "Sire, I will take the risk upon myself. I do not know fear."

So the Huntsman went into the wood with his Dog. Before long the Dog put up some game, and wanted to chase it; but hardly had he taken a few steps when he came to a deep pool, and could go no further. A naked arm appeared out of the water, seized him, and drew him down.

When the Huntsman saw this, he went back and fetched three men with pails to empty the pool. When they got to the bottom they found a Wild Man, whose body was as brown as rusty iron, and whose hair hung down over his face to his knees. They bound him with cords, and carried him away to the castle. There was great excitement over the Wild Man, and the King had an iron cage made for him in the courtyard. He forbade anyone to open the door of the cage on pain of death, and the Queen had to keep the key in her own charge.

After this, anybody could walk in the forest with safety.

The King had a little son eight years old, and one day he was playing in the courtyard. In his play his golden ball fell into the cage. The boy ran up, and said, "Give me back my ball."

"Not until you have opened the door," said the Wild Man.

"No, I can't do that," said the boy. "My father has forbidden it." Then he ran away.

Next day he came again, and asked for his ball. The Man said, "Open my door", but he would not.

On the third day the King went out hunting, and the boy came again, and said, "Even if I would, I could not open the door. I do not have the key."

Then the Wild Man said, "It is lying under your mother's pillow. You can get it easily."

The boy, who was very anxious to have his ball back, threw his scruples to the winds, and fetched the key. The door was very stiff, and he pinched his fingers in opening it. As soon as it was open the Wild Man came out, gave the boy his ball, and hurried away. The boy was now very frightened, and cried out, "Oh, Wild Man, don't go away, or I shall be beaten."

The Wild Man turned back, picked up the boy, put him on his shoulder, and walked hurriedly off into the wood.

When the King came home he saw the empty cage, and asked the Queen how it had come about. She knew nothing about it, and went to look for the key, which was of course gone. They called the boy, but there was no answer. The King sent people out into the fields to look for him, but all in vain; he was gone. The King easily guessed what had happened, and great grief fell on the royal household.

When the Wild Man got back into the depths of the dark forest he took the boy down off his shoulder, and said, "You will never see your father and mother again; but I will keep you here with me, because you had pity on me and set me free. If you do as you are told, you will be well treated. I have more treasures and gold than anybody in the world."

He made a bed of moss for the boy, on which he went to sleep. Next morning the Man led him to a spring, and said, "You see this golden well is bright and clear as crystal. You must sit by it, and take care that nothing falls into it, or it will be contaminated. I shall come every evening to see if you have obeyed my orders."

The boy sat down on the edge of the spring to watch it. Sometimes he would see a gold fish or a golden snake darting through it, and he guarded it well, so that nothing should fall into it. One day as he was sitting like this his finger, which he had caught in the Wild Man's cage, pained him so much that involuntarily he dipped it into the water. He drew it out very quickly, but saw that it was gilded, and although he tried hard to rub it off, it remained golden. In the evening the Wild Man, who was called Iron Hans came back. He looked at the boy, and said, "What has happened to the well today?"

"Nothing, nothing!" the boy answered, keeping his finger behind his back so that Iron Hans should not see it.

But he said, "You have dipped your finger into the water. It does not matter this time, but take care that nothing of the kind occurs again."

Early next morning the boy took his seat by the spring again to watch. His finger still hurt very much, and he put his hand up above his head. Unfortunately, in so doing, he brushed a hair into the well. He quickly took it out, but it was already gilded. When Iron Hans came in the evening, he knew very well what had happened.

"You have let a hair fall into the well," he said. "I will overlook it once more, but if it happens for the third time, the well will be polluted, and you can no longer stay with me."

On the third day the boy again sat by the well. He took good care not to move a finger, however much it might hurt. The time seemed very long to him as he looked at his face reflected in the water. As he bent over further and further to look into his eyes, his long hair fell over his shoulder right into the water. He started up at once, but not before his whole head of hair had become golden, and glittered like the sun. You may imagine how frightened the poor by was. He took his handkerchief and tied it over his head, so that Iron Hans would not see it. But he knew all about it before he came, and at once said, "Take that handkerchief off your head." Then all the golden hair tumbled out. The poor boy's excuses were no good. "You have not stood the test, and you can no longer stay here. You must go out into the world, and there you will learn the meaning of poverty. But as your heart is not bad, and as I wish you well, I will grant you one thing. When you are in great need go to the forest and cry 'Iron Hans,' and I will come and help you. My power is great, greater than you think, and I have gold and silver in abundance."

So the King's son left the forest, and wandered over trodden and untrodden paths till he reached a great city that he had never seen before. He tried to get work, but he could not find any. Besides, he knew no trade by which to make a living. At last he went to the castle and asked if they would employ him. The courtiers did not know what use they could make of him, but they were taken with his appearance, and said he might stay. At last the Cook took him into his service, and said he might carry wood and water for him, and sweep up the ashes.

One day, as there was no one else at hand, the Cook ordered him to carry the food up to the royal table. As he did not want his golden hair to be seen, the boy kept his cap on. Nothing of the sort had ever happened in the presence of the King before, and he said, "When you come into the royal presence, you must take your cap off."

"Alas, Sire," he said, "I cannot take it off, I have a bad wound on my head."

Then the King ordered the Cook to be called, and asked how he could take such a boy into his service, and ordered him to be sent away at once. But the Cook was sorry for him, and exchanged him with the Gardener's helper.

Now the boy had to dig and hoe, plant and water, in every kind of weather. One day in the summer, when he was working alone in the garden, it was very hot, and he took off his cap for the fresh air to cool his head. When the sun shone on his hair, it glittered so that the beams penetrated right into the Princess's room, and she sprang up to see what it was. She discovered the youth, and called to him, "Bring me a bouquet, young man."

He hurriedly put on his cap, picked a lot of wild flowers, and tied them up. On his way up to the Princess, the Gardener met him, and said, "How can you take such poor flowers to the Princess? Quickly cut another bouquet, and mind they are the choicest and rarest flowers."

"Oh no," said the youth. "The wild flowers have a sweeter scent, and will please her better."

As soon as he went into the room the Princess said, "Take off your cap. It is not proper for you to wear it before me."

He answered again, "I may not take it off because I

have a wound on my head."

But she took hold of the cap, and pulled it off, and all his golden hair tumbled out. It was quite a sight. He tried to get away, but she took hold of his arm, and gave him a handful of ducats. He took them, but cared nothing for the gold, and gave it to the Gardener.

Next day the Princess again called him to bring her a bunch of wild flowers, and when he brought it, she immediately clutched at his cap to pull it off; but he held it on with both hands. Again she gave him a handful of ducats, but he would not keep them, and gave them to the Gardener's children. The third day the same thing happened, but she could not take off his cap, and he would not keep the gold.

Not long after this the kingdom was invaded. The King assembled his warriors. He did not know whether they would be able to conquer his enemies or not, as they were very powerful and had a mighty army. Then the Gardener's assistant said, "I have been brought up to fight; give me a horse, and I will go too."

The others laughed, and said, "When we are gone, find one for yourself. We will leave one behind in the stable for you."

When they were gone, the boy went and got the horse out. It was lame in one leg, and hobbled along, humpety-hump, humpety-hump. Nevertheless, he mounted it and rode away to the dark forest. When he came to the edge of it, he called three times, "Iron Hans," as loud as he could, till the trees resounded with it.

The Wild Man appeared immediately, and said, "What do you want?"

"I want a strong horse to go to the war."

"You shall have it, and more besides."

The Wild Man went back into the wood, and before long a Groom came out, leading a fiery charger with snorting nostrils. Behind him followed a great body of warriors, all in armour, and their swords gleaming in the sun. The youth handed over his three-legged steed to the Groom, mounted the other, and rode away at the head of the troop.

When he approached the battlefield, a great many of the King's men had already fallen, and before long the remainder would have given in. Then the youth, at the head of his iron troop, charged, and bore down the enemy like a mighty wind, smiting everything which came in his way. They tried to fly, but the youth fell upon them, and did not stop while one remained alive.

Instead of joining the King, he led his troop straight back to the wood and called Iron Hans again.

"What do you want?" asked the Wild Man.

"Take back your charger and your troop, and give me back my three-legged steed."

His request was granted, and he rode his three-legged steed home.

When the King returned to the castle, his daughter met him and congratulated him on his victory.

"It was not I who won it," he said; "but a strange Knight, who came to my assistance with his troop." His daughter asked who the strange Knight was, but the King did not know, and said, "He pursued the enemy, and I have not seen him since."

She asked the Gardener about his assistant, but he laughed, and said, "He has just come home on his three-legged horse, and the others made fun of him, and said, 'Here comes our hobbler back again,' and asked which hedge he had been sleeping under. He answered, 'I did my best, and without me things would have gone badly.' Then they laughed at him more than ever."

The King said to his daughter, "I will give a great feast, lasting three days, and you shall throw a golden apple. Perhaps the unknown Knight will come among the others to try and catch it."

When notice was given of the feast, the youth went to the wood and called Iron Hans.

"What do you want?" he asked.

"I want to secure the King's golden apple," he said.

"It is as good as yours already," answered Iron Hans. "You shall have a tawny suit, and ride a proud chestnut."

When the day arrived, the youth took his place among the other Knights, but no one knew him. The Princess stepped forward and threw the apple among the Knights, and he was the only one who could catch it. As soon as he had it, he rode away.

On the second day Iron Hans fitted him out as a White

Knight, riding a gallant grey. Again he caught the apple; but he did not stay a minute, and, as before, hurried away.

The King now grew angry, and said, "This must not be. He must come before me and give me his name."

He gave an order that if the Knight made off again he was to be pursued and brought back.

On the third day the youth received from Iron Hans a black outfit, and a fiery black charger.

Again he caught the apple; but as he was riding off with it, the King's people chased him, and one came so near that he wounded him in the leg. Still he escaped, but his horse galloped so fast that his helmet fell off, and they all saw that he had golden hair. So they rode back, and told the King what they had seen.

Next day the Princess asked the Gardener about his assistant.

"He is working in the garden. The queer fellow went to the feast, and he only came back last night. He has shown my children three golden apples which he won."

The King ordered him to be brought before him. When he appeared he still wore his cap. But the Princess went up to him and took it off. Then all his golden hair fell out, and it was so beautiful that they were all amazed by it.

"Are you the Knight who came to the feast every day in a different colour, and who caught the three golden apples?" asked the King.

"Yes," he answered, "and here are the apples." He

took them out of his pocket and gave them to the King. "If you want further proof, here is the wound in my leg given me by your people when they pursued me. But I am also the Knight who helped you to conquer the enemy."

"If you can do such deeds, you are no Gardener's boy. Tell me who is your father?"

"My father is a powerful King, and I have plenty of gold—as much as I will ever want."

"I see very well," said the King, "that we owe you many thanks. Can I do anything to please you?"

"Yes," he answered, "indeed, you can. Give me your daughter to be my wife!"

The maiden laughed, and said, "He does not beat about the bush. I saw long ago that he was no Gardener's boy."

Then she went up to him and kissed him.

His father and mother came to the wedding, and they were full of joy, for they had long given up all hope of ever seeing their dear son again. As they were sitting at the wedding feast, the music suddenly stopped, the doors flew open, and a proud King walked in at the head of a great following. He went up to the Bridegroom, embraced him, and said, "I am Iron Hans, who was bewitched and changed into a Wild Man. But you have broken the spell and set me free. All that I have is yours."